I0783667

The Mystery of Hamish Grant

John Graeme

Clink Street

London | New York

Published by Clink Street Publishing 2016

Copyright © 2016

First edition.

The author asserts the moral right under the Copyright, Designs and Patents Act 1988 to be identified as the author of this work.

ISBN: 978-1-911110-28-6

Foreword to Hamish Grant

My late father, Graeme John Heldreich (1939–2013), came up with notion of *Hamish Grant* in the summer of 1987 during one of our many family holidays in Scotland, after a visit to the enigmatic and imposing Eilean Donan Castle on the west coast of Scotland, best known, perhaps, as a film location for the 1986 Hollywood blockbuster *Highlander*. My little sister Charlotte was maybe ten or eleven at the time, and was clearly enthralled by the magic and mystery of the place, which set our father's highly imaginative and creative brain whirring; and so, over the next few days, whilst driving around the scenic and rugged Scottish lochs and mountains, he began to construct the story that would become *The Mystery of Hamish Grant*. I recall even then being gripped by every twist and turn of the story, each of us, my two sisters and myself, coming up with appropriate names for characters and so on with Dad telling us the next chapter of the story each day as the holiday progressed.

Although Dad qualified as a dental surgeon, he was very much the polymath with interests in a wide range of subjects ranging from archaeology to zoology. He read thousands of books, including the Bible and *The Complete Works of Shakespeare*, and wrote many published articles on subjects as diverse as *Percussion Cap Conversions from Flintlock* to the *History of the Semiconductor*. He had already completed his first, soon to be, published work, *A History of the von Heldreich Family & their English Descendants*, and was the consummate *raconteur*; a skill which he employed with great passion and devilish wit, never more so than when it came to producing wonderment and awe on the faces of inquisitive and enrapt children.

As *Hamish Grant* was never published during Dad's lifetime it was my brother Edward who set about unearthing the original manuscript and putting together the book you see before you now. In particular, mention should be made of the wonderful illustrations drawn by Jonathan Wolstenholme, which, along with the text, bring the story so vividly to life. I do hope it brings as much thrilling joy to you, dear reader, as it brought to our family nearly three decades ago.

Jonnie Heldreich – May 2014

Chapter 1

Sarah stood in front of the huge stone fireplace, looking up at the portrait of Hamish Grant. Her eyes seemed drawn to the handsome boyish face, and as she studied it, she felt the little hairs on the nape of her neck prickle. A small shiver ran up her spine as if the room had suddenly become cold. She stared at the picture of the young lieutenant, her gaze held by the painted eyes. The droning of the guide's voice and the murmurs of the visitors seemed to get farther and farther away until she was aware of them no more.

Now, Sarah felt the heat coming from red-glowing blocks of peat in the great fireplace. She forced herself to look around the room. It looked both the same as a moment before but also, in some way, different. The tapestry bed cover was pulled half onto the floor and there was a reddish-brown stain on it, which she hadn't noticed before. Then she was looking up at Hamish Grant again. His blue eyes were staring straight into hers, with an urgent, pleading look.

Suddenly, a large pewter candlestick on the end of the oak mantelpiece moved slightly, rocked, then fell with a crash to the stone-flagged floor.

Mrs Forbes, the castle guide, had been describing a huge, carved oak chest, with a jigsaw of massive black, iron locks beneath the raised lid. When the candlestick hit the flagstones, the crowd around her parted as if by magic and she rushed across the room to where Sarah stood looking white and dazed.

"What on earth have you done, girl?" she cried. "I told everyone quite clearly at the beginning of the tour not to touch anything." She stooped and picked up the candlestick, examining the heavy metal base anxiously. "Thank goodness it isn't broken. What were you doing to knock such a heavy thing off the shelf? I suppose you picked it up to see how much it weighed?"

Sarah still looked dazed and confused. "I don't know what happened," she said eventually. "I think the heat of the fire made me feel faint. I must have put my hand out to stop myself falling and knocked it."

The guide looked at her oddly. "There is no fire," she said.

Sarah looked at the fireplace and felt a rush of disbelief turning to panic. Where, a moment ago, there had been glowing peat, the iron fire-basket was now filled with large fir cones. She looked up at the portrait, but the eyes gazed blankly into the distance. Sarah turned quickly, beginning to feel very frightened. The room was no longer as she had just seen it; the tapestry bedcover was back on the bed, and there was no sign of the large brown stain.

She turned to Mrs Forbes and stared at her, silent and trembling, her face white and drawn.

"She looks terrible," said a plump, motherly, woman. "I think she should go outside into the fresh air. Come on, love, I'll take you outside till you feel better."

"I'm her cousin," said Alison quickly, "I think I'd better take her home." She led Sarah by the arm through the door and along the passage to the top of the steep spiral staircase.

"Will you be all right going down the stairs?" she asked anxiously, "I don't think I could hold you if you fainted."

Sarah gazed at her with a strained look on her still white face and nodded.

Alison said, "I'll go first. You hang on to the handrope, and then if you fall, I can stop you."

The two girls made their way cautiously down the narrow stone steps, polished treacherously smooth over the centuries by hundreds of feet.

Holding on to Alison's hand, Sarah said, "I was sure there was a fire in the fireplace. I could feel the heat and I remember feeling sort of funny."

"Perhaps you'd been standing up for too long," Alison replied. "Let's go into the Tea Room and have a cup of tea and something to eat, then you'll feel better."

***

Sarah sat at a little table with a neat red and white check tablecloth. Alison threaded her way between the tables holding a brown plastic tray with a small pot of tea and two jam doughnuts.

When she had eaten a mouthful of cake and drunk some of the tea, Sarah felt the colour coming back to her cheeks and the sick feeling in her stomach went away.

"You're looking heaps better," Alison commented. "I said you would, didn't I?"

"I feel okay now," Sarah replied, "but I did feel dreadful. It was when I looked at Hamish Grant's picture; it was like he was staring at me and everything seemed to go very far away. I was really, really scared, I can tell you."

Alison grinned at her scornfully. "You mean you were scared by old Ma Forbes' story about the room being haunted. Come on; admit it! My God, what a wimp, frightened by a stupid ghost story. Wait till I tell Mum, she'll have hysterics."

"Don't you dare tell her, you rotten pig!" Sarah shouted, "I'll get you if you do!"

The whole room went quiet, as everyone turned and stared at her. The manageress gave her a steely look from behind the cash register, and Sarah blushed in embarrassment. Alison lowered her head and looked at her plate with a wicked grin and then laughed, spraying the table with bits of doughnut. Sarah glared at her cousin then slumped down furiously into her chair.

They sat in silence, Alison still studiously examining her plate, but out of the corner of her eye, Sarah saw her raise her eyes and give her her taunting grin again.

"You ratbag!" she hissed viciously. "I'll get you back for this." She aimed a rapid punch at Alison's arm. Alison whipped her hand away quickly, and her teacup went spinning over the tablecloth, leaving a soggy trail.

The manageress threw down the cloth she was holding and advanced across the room. "Right, you two! Out you go! I'm not having this sort of thing in here. It's a pity no one ever taught you how to behave properly."

They scuttled out of the Tea Room shamefaced. Once outside a furious argument ensued.

"It's a pity you can't take a joke," Alison said loftily. "Anyway it was you who knocked my tea over and got us chucked out."

"You started it! It was your fault, and you know it!" Sarah shouted.

"Oh, knickers! You attacked me because you're a wimpy little girl who's frightened of ghosts."

"Just you wait! I'll get you; see if I don't," Sarah spat. Looking wildly around, she bent down and picked up a stick. She hurled it at Alison as hard as she could, but Alison just laughed and dodged out of the way.

On the way back to the village, they walked on opposite sides of the road. Sarah strode, head up and aloof, trying to give the appearance of haughty disdain but Alison kept looking across, sniggering and pulling faces. Stung by her cousin's laughter, Sarah kicked furiously at stones on the road.

Chapter 2

It took about twenty minutes to walk home. Alison lived in a grey stone house near the edge of the village. It had a slate roof, and the upstairs rooms had sloping ceilings and dormer windows. The house was up a narrow lane off the main road and beyond the garden the hillside rose steeply, covered with purple heather and occasional clumps of silver birch.

Alison's bedroom had a fine view of the loch. From her window, she could see the scattered islands where it joined the sea and, on the other side of a shallow bay, the small headland from which a stone causeway led to the romantically grim tower of Craig Dubh Castle, built on a dark outcrop of rock in the sea-loch.

When they arrived, Sarah was still sulking. As they sat around the kitchen table, Alison started to relate the afternoon's events to her mother.

"Anyway, one stormy night in nineteen forty, he disappeared from his room in the tower and was never seen again," she said. "Some people think he was a spy who did a bunk because he knew he was going to be arrested, but it's still a big mystery. Old Ma Forbes says that his wife has refused to enter the room ever since and that people think the place is haunted. But the best bit was, it scared Sarah so much she nearly fainted when we went inside. I had to take her out and spend my own hard-earned money on tea and cakes to revive her."

Sarah looked down at the table, feeling embarrassed and furious with Alison. "That's not true!" she protested angrily, and she told her aunt what had happened to her.

Jean looked at her niece and felt a small flicker of concern as she saw the signs of distress on the girl's face. She loved her dead sister's daughter; so like Alison in many ways but more thoughtful and sensitive; kinder perhaps, than her own boisterous offspring.

She put her arm around Sarah's shoulders and hugged her. "Take no notice of her. She wouldn't see a ghost if it poked her with a stick. Lots of people have strange experiences. It just means you are a more receptive person – instead of having the sensitivity of a wart hog like Alison."

Comforted by her aunt's hug, Sarah smiled and poked her tongue out at Alison. "I really did think I saw a fire in the hearth, though. It was very hot and when I looked up, it was like he was looking straight at me. He seemed so sad that I'm sure something terrible must have happened to him."

"I reckon she's got a crush on Hamish Grant," said Alison. "It's probably the uniform," she considered. "Uniforms have that effect on some women, you know."

Her mother raised her eyebrows. "And what would you know about it?"

"Oh everybody knows that, it's a well-known fact. Anyway, I read it in a magazine at the dentist's."

"I think he should get a better class of magazine in the waiting room," her mother replied, smiling to herself. "Still, that's enough about that subject. I've got a good idea. How about we eat out this evening?"

Both girls brightened up immediately.

"Oh, great!" Alison enthused. "Can we go to the Hunter's Moon? I could kill for lasagne and profiteroles."

***

The evening passed very pleasantly, as the girls were friends again. When they returned to the house, it was quite late. The disturbing events of the day had left Sarah feeling drained and once in bed she quickly fell asleep.

***

The full moon bathed the room with a bright light and through the open window came the sound of the waves breaking on the shore. She had not been asleep very long when she felt she was back in the room at the top of the tower. She saw the massive stone fireplace with the red-glowing peat fire and her eyes were drawn upwards to the face of Hamish Grant. He was looking straight at her with a look of desperate sadness and tragedy. As her eyes were held by his, he seemed to grow larger and nearer until he filled her vision. Sarah heard, as if from very far away, a voice calling her name.

"I'm here," she answered out loud, moving her head from side to side as she slept.

The voice became very close, "Help me, Sarah! Help me, Sarah!"

She opened her eyes wide and slowly rose from the bed. Still asleep, she moved to the window and looked out across the silver, moonlit loch towards the distant, black mass of the castle on its rock. The image of Hamish Grant seemed to float away from her towards the castle, and his voice became fainter until she could only hear a sort of echo in her mind, "Help me, Sarah! Help me!"

"I will," she cried desperately, "I will help you!"

Suddenly, the light clicked on. Alison sat up with a start and gazed open-mouthed at the girl by the window.

"What on earth's going on?" Alison's mother asked sharply. Seeing Sarah standing dazed, she quickly crossed the room and took her by the shoulders. "I think you must've had a bad dream," she said, sitting on the foot of the bed and holding Sarah close to her.

"I saw Hamish Grant again," Sarah mumbled, still confused. She started to tremble, and her voice rose to a wail. "He was here – *in the room*!"

"Hush, darling. It was just a dream," Jean said, hugging her and stroking her hair. "Why don't you come and sleep in my bed for the rest of the night and it won't come again?"

She led Sarah to the door.

"Can't I come as well?" said Alison, scrambling rapidly out of bed. "I don't want to stay here if there are any ghosts."

"There are no ghosts," said her mother sharply. "She just had a bad dream, but come if you must."

Sarah climbed into the huge, old-fashioned, double bed and snuggled up to her aunt, who put her arms around her. Slowly she stopped trembling and gradually fell asleep while Jean Frazer lay wide awake in the darkness. She could not shake off the peculiar feeling that something sinister and frightening was happening to her niece.

Chapter 3

The bright sun was streaming through the window as Sarah woke to find herself alone in the unfamiliar bed. From where she lay, she could see tiny white sheep on the purple heather covered hillside and a single, small, cotton-wool cloud in the strip of clear blue sky above.

From below came the sound of the radio, accompanied by the clatter of crockery as her aunt prepared breakfast. The wonderful smell of frying bacon and eggs, mingled with coffee and toast, wafted upwards from the kitchen. She sat up and swung her feet to the floor. Barefoot she padded in her nightdress to the stairs and down to the kitchen.

Jean looked up from the plate she was taking from the oven. "That was well-timed; I was just about to call you. How do you feel this morning?"

"Oh, I'm all right, but why was I in your bed?"

"You were seeing ghosts again in the night," Alison answered, with her mouth full. "And you were sleep-walking. Frightened me to death, yelling and shouting like that."

Jean glared at her tactless daughter and frowned a warning.

"I wasn't sleep-walking and shouting, was I?" Sarah asked Jean indignantly.

"Oh yes, you were," Alison began belligerently. A swipe of her mother's hand silenced her.

"It was just a bad dream," her aunt reassured her gently.

"I expect all the excitement yesterday caused it. Anyway, let's forget about it now and eat our breakfast before it gets cold."

***

It was Jean's day for 'Meals on Wheels', when she helped to deliver cooked lunches to elderly people; shortly afterwards, she left the girls to their own devices.

They dragged the sun-beds into the garden to sunbathe. At first, they chatted in a desultory fashion but the warmth soon made them drowsy, and they just lay soaking in the sun's rays.

Sarah closed her eyes. She could hear the sighing of the wind in the tops of the tall pine trees in the garden, and gradually it began to sound like the waves on the shore of the loch. In her mind's eye, she pictured the moonlit castle in her dream and the echo of the pleading voice seemed to come back to her.

"He's asking me to help him," she said suddenly. "I think something horrible happened to him, and he can't rest until it's put right."

"Who are you talking about?" Alison sat up startled; "Oh God, not that again? Haven't we had enough of Hamish Grant after last night? If you keep going on about it, you'll end up going funny."

"I don't care. I think his soul is calling to me for help. I'm not frightened any more because he's not evil, only very sad."

"I think the theory about him being a spy and being picked up from the sea-loch in the dead of night by a submarine is far more likely," said her cousin in disgust. "I think he skipped out when the old spying got too dangerous and is alive and well in Hamburg as Herr Schmidt or somesuch. You really will have to stop acting like a romantic little schoolgirl, or I'll be the one who goes barmy."

"I don't think he would've been a spy," Sarah said dreamily. "He looked so dishy in his uniform; come on agree with me – wasn't he just too handsome? I wish I could find out more about his disappearance."

"The Navy probably did find out," said Alison. "It was probably covered up to prevent a scandal. These rich old families can always pull strings."

"I think I'll go and see Sergeant Campbell in the village and ask him if he knows anything," Sarah mused.

"Before his time," replied Alison. "Anyway, why should he tell you, even if he knows anything?"

"I'll tell him I have to do a school project on my holiday and that I'm doing one on the mystery of Craig Dubh Castle."

"You better not let Mum find out. She'll do her nut after last night," Alison answered rudely.

***

They lay in the sun for nearly an hour. Alison dozed with her eyes closed behind her fashionable sunglasses, surfacing now and again to swat irritably at an importunate wasp.

Sarah lay quietly, deep in thought. "How about it, then?" she asked eventually.

Alison raised her head enquiringly. "How about what?"

"How about going to see Sergeant Campbell?"

"Oh God! Can't you just forget about all that Hamish Grant rubbish," responded Alison impatiently. "It's getting very boring. And the answer's no! I don't want to waste the whole day just trekking around asking people about stupid Hamish Grant. Why are you so fascinated by him anyway?"

"I just think it's a fantastic mystery, and it would be great to solve it," Sarah replied defensively. "Anyway I am going to do it as my project. It will be much better than anyone else's boring holidays."

"I still think you've got an adolescent crush on him," Alison jeered. "It's a bit sick getting all sloppy over a dead man."

Sarah glared at her. "I thought you said he wasn't dead, and I don't care what you think anyway," she snapped. "Besides, it won't take all day. Why do you always have to exaggerate everything? You never want to do what I want, only what you want to do. If you're too mean to come with me, I'll go on my own."

Alison shrugged, bad temperedly. "Oh, all right then, let's get it over with. It'll be a complete waste of time because Mr Campbell will just tell you to clear off, anyway."

They dressed, got their bikes out of the shed and set off. Alison, with a sullen and uncooperative look on her face, kept riding behind forcing Sarah to stop every so often until she had caught up. When they reached the Police House, Sarah realised that the sergeant's van wasn't there.

"See, I told you it was a waste of time," Alison said belligerently. "He's out somewhere, and he probably won't be back for hours."

"Well, I'm going to ask," said Sarah defiantly, opening the blue wicket gate.

She entered the porch door, which led into a small bare room lined with notice boards covered with leaflets and posters. On the opposite wall was a blue door with a brass Yale lock and, beside it, a blue painted hatchway with a sliding door. She pressed the bell-push marked 'Press for Attention'.

After a few moments, the hatch slid open to reveal the plump, pleasant face of Mrs Campbell. "Good morning, girls," she smiled, "what can I do for you today, then?"

"Can you tell me if Sergeant Campbell will be back soon?" Sarah asked, losing some of her nervousness.

"Oh, he's away round the hill farms today," the sergeant's wife replied. "He won't be back until lunchtime at least. Some of the farmers are having sheep stolen."

"I'll come back later, then," said Sarah, disappointed. She wondered how she would persuade Alison to come back again.

"What did you want to see him about? Is there anything wrong or urgent?"

"Oh, no, it's not urgent," Sarah replied hurriedly. "I just wanted some information about something."

"Well, if you tell me what you want to know, I can maybe tell you myself," said Mrs Campbell kindly, "or I can ask him when he comes in."

Sarah told her carefully rehearsed story about the school

project. The sergeant's wife opened the blue door and came into the little room, shaking her head doubtfully. "I don't know if he'll know much about it, my dear," she said slowly. "It was all well before our time here. Everybody knows the story of course, but I don't think he'll be able to add much more to it."

"I just thought he might know what was found out at the time. Just in case, the police had any suspicions about what really happened which weren't made public."

"I'm sure they didn't find a thing. I'll ask him when he comes in for lunch and see what he says, but I wouldn't be too hopeful. If you come back at about two o'clock, you might catch him before he goes out again. If not, I'll tell you what he said."

After thanking the sergeant's wife, the girls stood outside, uncertain what to do until two o'clock.

"I told you it was a waste of time, didn't I?" said Alison a little more kindly now. Although she was impatient and inclined to be sharp-tongued, she hated not to be friends with Sarah. "If the police or the Navy had discovered anything, it would have come out by no"But, you said yourself that rich families always got scandals covered up."

"Oh, I don't know," Alison responded wearily, "I just don't want to argue about it any more. What can we do until two o'clock? I'm starving. Let's go home and get something to eat."

Chapter 4

Alison concocted her favourite lunch of beefburgers, baked beans and potato crisps, after which the two cousins sprawled in front of the TV.

The programme ended; she stood up and said. "It's ten to two now. Let's get going and see if the sergeant's come back – if we must."

The van was parked outside the Police House when they arrived. Sarah felt a little flutter of nervousness. She was sure that Mr Campbell would see through her story about the project. She rang the bell and after a few moments, the sergeant opened the hatch. He had his uniform jacket off, and Sarah could see his half-eaten meal on the table.

"Oh, I'm sorry to disturb your lunch," she said quickly, "I'll come back later."

"Don't worry about that, lassie," replied the sergeant, reaching across to open the door. "Come away in, if you don't mind watching me eat. I've only just now got back."

The girls perched on the edge of the sofa while the police officer sat down at the table to finish his lunch of stew and dumplings.

"You wanted to know about the Hamish Grant business, then?" he said looking at Sarah. He was a burly man with a kind face, but Sarah realised that he had the sort of direct watchful look all police officers seemed to acquire, and she felt uncomfortable as she repeated her story about the school project.

"I wondered if the police or the Navy ever had any suspicions about it which were never made public?" she asked.

Sergeant Campbell shook his head. "Not that I've ever heard of anyway, but it was well before my time. Willie Jamieson was the village constable in those days, why don't you go and ask him?"

"Do you mean he's still alive?" Sarah asked, surprised.

The sergeant laughed. "I shouldn't let him hear you say that. He's not that old you know, only in his mid-sixties I should think."

Alison was suddenly interested. "Does he live near?"

"He has a cottage near Glenmore," Mrs Campbell replied. "It's about three miles mind, but you should be able to manage well enough on your bikes."

"Do you think he'll mind if we visit him?" Sarah asked.

Mrs Campbell laughed. "I think he'll be glad to see some new faces. It's so far out of the way up there, and he's been on his own since his wife died."

They said their thanks and rose to leave. The sergeant got up from the table and accompanied them to the door.

"Let me know if you solve the mystery," he said, smiling, "I could do with a promotion."

***

It was a hard ride to Glenmore, and the sky had clouded over with the threat of rain. Following the directions they had been given, they found the cottage owned by the retired constable. Willie Jamieson was in the garden pruning his roses. He straightened up when Sarah introduced herself and Alison and listened as Sarah told her story once again.

"Well, lassie," he said when she had finished, "I don't know there's that much to tell. Still, why don't you both come in and have a cup of tea, and I'll see what I can remember after all this time."

They sat in the tiny old-fashioned parlour until Mr Jamieson returned, carrying a tray loaded with fine china cups and saucers, a matching teapot and a plate of chocolate digestive biscuits.

As they talked and drank, it soon became apparent there was absolutely nothing at all wrong with the constable's memory of the events of all those years before.

"I was very young and keen, and it was the first really sensational thing that had ever happened on my patch. As a matter of fact it's about the only exciting thing that ever happened around here," he smiled. "That's why folk all remember it."

"I don't know exactly what happened on the night he disappeared," said Sarah. "I mean, when was he last seen and where was his wife when he disappeared?"

"Well, it was the night before Hamish Grant was due to rejoin his ship after a week's leave. There was a very bad southwesterly gale, I remember, which brought down a lot of trees. They had a live-in cook and a maid who served dinner at seven o'clock, but they lived in a flat over the gatehouse and didn't see either of the couple after that.

"Mrs Grant was the last person to see him, but she apparently decided to go and see her mother at the family home a couple of miles away and stayed the night because of the storm. The maid found him gone in the morning, but at first thought he'd left early to rejoin his ship. Nobody suspected anything until the Navy telephoned the castle to find out why he hadn't returned from leave. Then they rang me at the Police House and asked me to go and see Mrs Grant, who was still up at Kilmore House."

"What happened then?" Alison asked, fascinated.

"Well, first I searched the castle with the maid and the cook. Mrs Grant was too upset to come with us and wouldn't move out of the entrance hall. I called the doctor to her, and he took her back to Kilmore House and gave her a sedative. Later in the day, two officers arrived from the naval base, and an inspector arrived from Fort William with my local sergeant and a couple of constables. There was a big search, of course, in case he'd got lost in the storm, but Mrs Grant had taken their only car and we soon confirmed that the local taxi hadn't been used.

He'd apparently just vanished into thin air. The only trace of him that was ever found was when his uniform was discovered floating in the loch about a month later."

"Did the police or the Navy ever have any suspicions about what happened, perhaps that they couldn't prove?" asked Sarah.

He shook his head. "Not a thing. They all drew a complete blank."

Something in his expression made Sarah say intuitively, "Did you have any suspicions yourself?"

He looked at her a little sharply, surprised by the girl's perception. "Aye, well I had my own ideas," he said grimly, "but let's say that the powers-that-be weren't too interested in the opinions of a green young constable."

"What did you think happened?" Sarah felt the excitement of discovery rising within her.

The old constable looked at her eager young face for a long moment, then shook his head. "I can't tell you that, lassie. I'm afraid there are such things as the law of slander for one thing, and I don't believe in spreading idle gossip." Sarah's face fell, and seeing her disappointment, he added, "Let's just say that certain people's stories didn't ring quite true to me."

"But what about the spy story?" Alison asked. "Did you believe in the submarine and all that?"

"No, lassie, I didn't," he answered firmly. "Hamish Grant was a fine boy and was no spy. That tale was just war fever, like the stories about German parachutists dressed as nuns."

"Well, what do you think happened to him?" Alison persisted.

The elderly policeman looked at her unsmiling. "I think someone did away with him."

***

On the ride home, they met Sergeant Campbell's van just outside the village. He flashed his headlights and stopped next to them, winding down his window.

"Did you find Willie Jamieson, then?" he smiled.

Sarah nodded, "Yes thanks, Mr Campbell."

"Did he tell you anything interesting?"

"Mr Jamieson thinks that Hamish Grant was murdered," said Sarah.

The sergeant looked at her in surprise. "Does he now?" he said quietly.

"Yes. And he knows who did it," gabbled Alison breathlessly. "Only he can't prove it, and nobody would ever listen to him."

The sergeant looked at her without expression and after a moment he said, almost to himself, "I might pop in and see Willie next time I'm up that way. It's a long time since we had a chat."

The police van drove off just as it began to rain hard. By the time the girls reached home, they were wet through.

Jean was in the kitchen preparing dinner. "Where on earth have you been?"

Sarah shot her cousin a quick frown of warning. "We went on a long ride as far as Glenmore."

"Well, you left the sun-beds out in the rain as usual. You'd better go and get out of those wet things immediately and have a hot bath before you catch cold."

The girls bathed and ate their dinner in their dressing gowns, with towels round their hair like giant turbans. The rain was still falling heavily so after dinner they watched television for the rest of the evening before going to bed.

When Jean went up herself, she opened the door of the girls' room and checked on Sarah, who was sleeping peacefully.

***

Sometime later the rain stopped, and the clouds started to break up. Outside the dark and sleeping house, the water dripped steadily from the shrubbery, and the sodden lawn gleamed slightly in the intermittent moonlight. A large cloud slowly cleared the face of the moon, and the loch was bathed in silver light. Up at the front bedroom window, a white figure stood motionless, gazing across to the dark mass of the castle on its black rock.

Chapter 5

After breakfast the girls discussed the mystery while they got dressed, safely out of earshot of Alison's mother, who was in the garden, picking flowers.

"You know what struck me as odd about the story?" Alison mused as she sprawled on her bed.

Sarah looked up from brushing her hair. "What?"

"It's very odd Mrs Grant went to visit her mother on the last night of his leave."

Sarah looked at her uncertainly. "What do you mean?"

"Oh, come on Little Miss Innocent!" Alison giggled, "handsome young officer, could be going off to his death in battle, and she goes to her mother's?"

"You've just got a dirty little mind; not everybody's sex mad like you."

"Maybe not," smirked Alison, "but it still seems pretty odd behaviour to me."

"Perhaps that's what Constable Jamieson meant about people's stories not adding up?" Sarah said thoughtfully.

"I reckon they'd had a row, and she went home to mother, most likely," Alison decided, rolling off the bed.

***

For the next hour or so Jean found chores for the two girls to do around the house, after which they decided to ride down to the village shop for an ice-cream and a few items Jean needed. Coming out of the shop, they met Mrs Campbell, who greeted them warmly.

"So you found old Willie all right yesterday? Did he tell you all you wanted to know?"

"Yes, he was very nice," Sarah replied. "He told us all about how the disappearance was discovered and the search and about Mrs Grant."

"Aye, she's an odd one by all accounts, she shut herself away in that house all these years except when she goes to London, or abroad for the sun in winter."

"Didn't she ever remarry?" asked Alison.

Mrs Campbell's face assumed a disdainful expression. "Not her. Some round here say she only married Hamish Grant for the chance to be the laird's wife, as she was only the daughter of a jumped-up grocer from Glasgow."

Sarah was puzzled. "I thought her parents lived at Kilmore House?"

"Oh, they did, my dear, but her father only bought it a few years before the war when he sold his chain of grocery shops in Glasgow. I suppose he thought buying Kilmore House would make him a gentleman. Mind you, it was Moira Grant's mother who was the real social climber. People say she pushed her daughter into marrying young Hamish. The Grants were a very old family, with the estate and the castle, even though they weren't well off otherwise. It was a marriage of old man Pringle's money and the Grant name really."

"How awful," said Sarah innocently.

"Well, to give her her due, Moira Pringle, as she was, was said to be a very good-looking girl in those days. I expect young Hamish was quite taken with her. It doesn't take much to fool a man when the face is pretty," she sniffed.

"Do you think Mrs Grant would talk to me about the mystery?" Sarah asked.

"Good gracious me, no!" Mrs Campbell exclaimed. "She never has anything to do with anybody nowadays."

"Oh, that's a blow, I thought I might go and see her."

"No, dear, I should stay well away from there if I were you. I think you really would be sent packing with a flea in your ear."

"I suppose you're right," said Sarah in a disappointed voice. "In any case, it would be a terrible cheek."

"You could always go and see Annie Logan," Mrs Campbell volunteered encouragingly.

"Who's Annie Logan?" asked Alison.

"She was the maid at the castle, of course. It was Annie who found the laird gone in the morning and his bed not slept in."

"You mean she's still alive too?" Sarah marvelled.

Mrs Campbell smiled. "Yes of course she is; she was only a slip of a girl at the beginning of the war. There was just the two of them at the castle, her and the old cook, but she died years ago."

"Does she live far from here?" Alison asked with a resigned note in her voice.

"Not too far, dear. She has a cottage at Coinach on the Fort William road. It's the first one on the right just before you get to the village. You can't miss it."

The girls thanked the sergeant's wife, who went into the village shop.

"It looks like we're in for another marathon ride," Alison grumbled. "I shall have legs like tree trunks if there's much more of this."

"They're already like tree trunks," said Sarah, rapidly avoiding a vicious punch. "We'd better go this afternoon," she added, "your mum will be suspicious if we don't go back for lunch. Anyway, we've got these things from the shop, I don't want to cart them all that way."

After they had eaten lunch, the girls told Jean that they were going on another bike ride.

"You're doing a lot of riding all of a sudden," she said. "Still, I suppose all the fresh air and exercise must be doing you good."

They rode down to the main road and turned left towards Fort William. The road took them round the shore of the loch, and as they passed the castle, Sarah stopped and stood looking across the causeway.

"Come on," Alison called impatiently as she rode past. A car driver hooted as he waited to turn into the car park. Still looking at the castle, Sarah slowly started to ride on. It was a hard uphill slog through the pass for the next couple of miles, but once over the top, the road ran quite gently downwards as the hills widened into a long glen.

They got off their bikes to rest. Alison bent over, gasping for breath.

"At least, we'll be able to whizz down there on the way back," she panted.

Coinach was about a mile farther along the glen. It comprised little more than a straggling group of cottages, a post box and a telephone box. They found Annie Logan's house easily. It was a single storey cottage of whitewashed stone with a roof of grey slate. At the front was a little wooden porch with a corrugated iron roof. There was a tiny garden, with a wire fence, in which were growing cabbages and beans on sticks. Each side of the door there was a wooden tub, bright with geraniums and begonias.

The door was answered by a small, middle-aged woman with grey hair tied in a bun at the back of her neck. She was wearing a flour-covered apron, and the girls could smell the delicious aroma of baking. Sarah introduced herself and repeated her story once again.

Mrs Logan listened to her doubtfully, anxious to get back to her oven. "I don't think I can help you, my dear; it's all dead and past now."

Sarah longed to tell her it was far from over until Hamish Grant's soul was at peace, but she realised it would sound very strange.

"Please, Mrs Logan, anything you can tell me will be a big help."

"It's just that I'm very busy at the moment," Annie replied, looking over her shoulder at the oven.

"We've come such a long way," said Alison quickly, anxious their journey would not be for nothing.

"Who is it, Annie?" a man's voice called from inside the cottage.

Half turning, Annie said over her shoulder, "It's just two girls from Kilmore wanting to know about the young laird disappearing."

"Well, ask them in for a cup of tea," the man suggested cheerfully.

Mrs Logan stepped back and held the door wide, smiling. "Come away in, then, girls."

The door led straight into the kitchen. Mr Logan sat in an old armchair in the far corner with a newspaper on his lap. His pipe lay in an ashtray on the arm of the chair and propped against the wall were two crutches.

Mrs Logan sat the girls at the big wooden table and began to put out cups and saucers.

"Would you fancy some fresh scones with raspberry jam?"

"Yes, please," they both chorused at once. Alison tried not to salivate.

Mr Logan accepted a cup of tea from his wife. "How did you get up here from Kilmore?"

"We rode here on our bikes," Sarah replied.

"My word that's a good long pull," he answered. "It's a wonderful thing to be young and strong with the use of your legs. What brings you all this way, then?"

Sarah repeated her story about the project.

"Aye, well, you've certainly come to the right place," he told her wickedly. "There's nobody like Annie for all the gossip."

"I certainly do not gossip, you old devil," retorted his wife smiling at her husband.

Sarah and Alison smiled happily at the man and woman.

"Can you tell me about the night Hamish Grant disappeared?" asked Sarah.

Mrs Logan pulled out a wooden chair from the table and sat down with her tea.

"Yes, well, let me see now. It was a very bad night," she began. "Mary and me did the laird's dinner, and we served it to them as usual in the dining room, and then after we had cleared away and done the washing-up, we went up to our flat over the gatehouse. I was going to go out and see Bill, who was my young man then," she looked across at Mr Logan, who smiled, "but the weather was so bad I decided to stay in and listen to the wireless with Mary."

"So you didn't see either Mr or Mrs Grant again that night?" Alison queried.

She shook her head sadly. "No, and I never saw the poor young laird again. Nobody did. It was such a shame, he was such a bonny young man."

Sarah leaned forward. "So what happened next?"

"Well, about ten o'clock, I heard the gate being opened; I looked out of the window, and I saw Mrs Grant get into the car and drive off."

"Was she on her own?"

"Oh yes, I could see into the car quite clearly, as it went over the causeway. There was just the one person in it."

"Weren't you surprised to see her going out at that time, in the middle of a gale I mean?" Alison asked curiously.

Annie nodded. "Yes, in a way, but Mary and me thought they'd had another row, and she'd stormed off in a temper again."

"They often had rows, then?" asked Sarah.

"Oh, yes. The young laird was a lovely chap, but he was very stubborn, and she had a vile temper if she didn't get her own way. Mary always said she'd been spoiled by her mother and father. Used to getting everything she wanted at the snap of her fingers."

"It sounds as if you didn't like her very much," Sarah commented.

"She was a nasty little minx if the truth is told. Neither Mary nor me would've stayed on if it hadn't been for her husband. She used to order us around as if we were dogs when he was away."

"Why did you think they had had a row on that night?" Alison asked her.

"Well, for one thing, they weren't talking to each other

much when we served dinner. You could cut the atmosphere with a knife, as they say."

"What happened in the morning?" Sarah asked.

"Well, at about six o'clock, I took the tea tray up to the room. It was earlier than usual because Mr Grant was due back at his ship. I knocked and went in, but the laird wasn't there, and the bed hadn't been slept in. At first, I thought he must have gone back early without wanting to wake us up, but then I remembered Mrs Grant had taken the car."

"Couldn't he have called a taxi?" Alison queried.

Mrs Logan shook her head. "There was only the one taxi in Kilmore in those days, and old Angus would never have turned out on such a night, not even for the laird. Besides, he would have sounded his horn like he always did, and we would have heard."

"What did you do then?" Sarah urged.

"Well, I went and told Mary, and we looked around but he wasn't in the castle, so in the end we decided to telephone Mrs Grant up at Kilmore House, but the storm had brought their telephone line down, and we couldn't get through. Later on, the Navy rang asking where Mr Grant was, so we telephoned the Police House to ask the constable if he could go up to Kilmore House and see Mrs Grant. Anyhow, the Navy had already rung him, and he was already on his way. Later on, the constable brought Mrs Grant back to the castle, and we searched the place from top to bottom; all of us except her 'ladyship', who we had to call the doctor to." "And nobody ever found any clues?" Alison wondered.

"Not a thing, it was just as if he had vanished into thin air."

"Couldn't he have gone out without you hearing him, say – when you were asleep?"

"Well, I suppose he could've but it was a terrible storm, and I can't see why he would."

Mr Logan had been sitting quietly smoking his pipe, while listening to his wife retelling the familiar story. He cleared his throat and put his pipe down.

"In any case, there was a search for three days afterwards; we went all round the loch and up the roads in every direction." He glanced down at his lap. "Of course, I had my legs in those days; I used to walk for miles."

"Bill was a forester until he was called up for the Navy," Annie explained. "He went back to it after the war but his back was broken when a log rolled on him."

Sarah was horrified. "Oh, I am sorry."

"Don't you worry about it, lassie," he reassured her. "It was more than ten years ago now; life goes on somehow."

Sarah thought it was time they went and thanked the couple for their help and hospitality.

Mrs Logan patted her hand. "That's quite all right, my dear. It's always a pleasure to see new faces and have a chat. Quite a mystery though, isn't it? I don't suppose we shall ever know what happened."

Mr Logan prodded his pipe towards her. "You haven't told her your pet theory yet."

Annie smiled and flapped her hand at his teasing.

"What was your theory about?" asked Alison.

"Well, it sounds silly really, but I thought, at first, that he might have been leaning out of the window and got sucked out by a gust of wind and washed away in the loch."

"Why?" asked Sarah astonished.

"Because…later, when I went into the laird's bedroom that old tapestry bedspread and the rug on the floor were damp, as if the rain had come in the window; silly of me really because the window was closed and the rest of the floor wasn't wet. Funny though," she finished thoughtfully.

"And they found his uniform in the loch a few weeks later," Mr Logan added. "Although they never found his body, I reckon he must have fallen into the loch somehow, there's no other explanation."

The girls repeated their thanks and set off home. Although the slope was gentle, it was long and they had to stop for a rest when they reached the top of the pass. They sat on a large boulder at the viewpoint, with the whole panorama of the loch and the castle spread out below them. Sarah sat silently staring at the castle.

"Mr Logan's right," said Alison, "he must have fallen in the loch somehow."

Sarah didn't answer.

"Don't you think so?"

"He wouldn't be asking me for help if it had just been an accident," Sarah said quietly. "Something terrible must have happened to him. I think he was murdered like Constable Jamieson thought."

"But all this asking for help is just your imagination. I don't believe that spirits ask people for help. Why pick on you anyway after all these years? Why not somebody else a long time ago?"

"I think he's tried, lots of times before," Sarah replied firmly. "Don't you remember the room is supposed to be haunted? I think that's because he's tried to contact other people."

"I'm sorry, but I still think you're imagining it all. I think the answer to the mystery is he somehow drowned in the loch."

"Well, what about Constable Jamieson then?" asked Sarah, defensively. "He thought he'd been murdered."

"Yes, but that could just be sour grapes because no one would listen to his pet theory. Remember there was an inspector and a sergeant on the case and he was only a junior constable."

Sarah shook her head. "It's no use, I think he never left the castle and he's still there somewhere. I just know he wants me to go back to the castle and find him. I'm going to go tomorrow and that's that."

Alison felt a sensation of fear in her stomach. "You know Mum won't let you after all the business with the dreams and sleep-walking and stuff."

Sarah looked at her defiantly. "Well, we won't tell her and then she won't know, will she?"

"I don't know why you say 'we'," Alison told her emphatically. "I'm certainly going nowhere near the place, and if you do, I shall tell Mum." She mounted her bike and rode off down the steep hill. Sarah hesitated then followed.

***

That evening they hardly spoke to each other. Jean, unused to the quiet, deduced that they had quarrelled and tried to reconcile them but shrugged and gave up when neither girl would respond. They went to bed in silence and soon fell asleep.

In the early hours of the morning, something woke Alison. Hearing a sound, she turned her head. Her eyes opened wide and she gasped when she saw a white clad figure standing by the window. At that moment, Sarah turned and glided unseeingly past her and returned to bed. Alison shot down under the bedclothes and pulled the pillow over her head, her heart beating so hard it shook her body.

Chapter 6

The following morning at breakfast, the girls were still not speaking.

Sarah looked down at her plate to avoid meeting her cousin's eye. She was desperately hoping Alison would not carry out her threat to tell her aunt about her plan. She decided to get Alison alone after breakfast and try to persuade her to at least keep quiet, even if she would not accompany her to the castle.

Alison glared at Sarah. She was sure she ought to tell her mother about Sarah sleep-walking in the night, and about her intention to return to the castle. Alison was very worried by her cousin's obsession with Hamish Grant.

"It must be preying on her mind," she thought, "or she wouldn't keep on sleep-walking." Although she sensibly rejected thoughts of any supernatural explanation, deep down she had been very frightened, seeing Sarah in her trance-like state.

She tried to reason out the cause of Sarah's behaviour. She thought it quite possible that losing her mother still affected Sarah's state of mind. She remembered reading somewhere that occurrences of things like poltergeists often seemed to involve disturbed young girls. It didn't comfort her much, however, to think that a possible alternative to the supernatural was that her much-loved cousin was mentally disturbed.

She made up her mind she would get Sarah alone and face her with an ultimatum. "If she doesn't give up all this stuff about Hamish Grant, I'm definitely going to tell Mum," she told herself and felt much better about the situation.

Jean noticed the two girls were still not their normal friendly selves and she made further efforts to reconcile them over breakfast. Since neither wanted her to know the real reason for their quarrel, they were equally unresponsive to her efforts. With a shrug, she gave up trying, feeling sure whatever it was would soon blow over.

That afternoon, she was due to attend a committee meeting of one of the charities she worked for. She spent the morning, with Alison and Sarah, giving the house a thorough and long overdue cleaning and so inadvertently prevented them from speaking privately until after she had gone.

Sarah sat with her elbows on the kitchen table resting her chin on her hands while Alison was making a mug of coffee. She didn't know how to start trying to persuade Alison to go with her to the castle, so she sat silently, looking down at the table. She was afraid even bringing up the subject would provoke an immediate refusal, or worse, cause Alison to carry out her threat to tell her mother about the plan.

Alison, for her part, felt just as tongue-tied and awkward. She sat down at the table with her coffee and without looking at Sarah said, "Did you know you were sleep-walking again last night?"

Sarah looked up quickly at her cousin, quite shocked. "I wasn't, was I? You're making it up."

"No I'm not, matey," Alison replied indignantly. "You gave me a hell of a shock when I woke up and saw you gliding around like Lady Macbeth."

"But, I couldn't have been, surely? I don't remember anything. Why didn't you wake me up?"

"People don't remember sleep-walking, stupid," said Alison scathingly. "You didn't remember anything the first night you did it either. Anyway, you're not supposed to wake sleep-walkers up," she added, anxious not to admit that she had been too terrified to do anything other than hide under the bedclothes.

"Have you told your mum?"

"Not yet, but I'm going to if you don't pack this Hamish Grant business in."

"Oh, no! Please don't," Sarah pleaded. "I've got to go back to the castle and see if I can discover anything; it can't do any harm, surely, and I promise to give up if nothing comes of it."

"No!" I've been worried to death about you since last night. You're absolutely obsessed by this stupid business, and I'm really afraid you might be going loopy. How do you think I would feel if I encouraged you to go on with it and then you had to be locked up in the funny-farm?"

"Oh, I'm not going loony. Don't be ridiculous," Sarah retorted angrily but felt a small quiver of anxiety run through her because whatever it was that had been happening to her was certainly not normal. The thought made her speak even more aggressively. "Look I just want to visit the place once more and you're being bang out of order, threatening to run to your mother like a little sneak."

"No I'm not!" shouted Alison. "You will just go on and on finding more excuses. It's unhealthy and dangerous to be so wrapped up in something so weird. I would never forgive myself if I didn't try and stop you and then something happened to you."

"You're being quite ridiculous," said Sarah loftily. "And anyway, you can't stop me going on my own. Run and tell tales to your mother if you must but she won't be back until teatime and that'll be too late."

"Please, don't go!" Alison felt hot tears start in her eyes. "What good will it do anyway? What could you see that the police and hundreds of others haven't seen in all this time?"

"I have to go," said Sarah, She didn't say she expected Hamish Grant to show her what others had failed to see. She realised this would only serve to confirm Alison's worst fears about her sanity. She had spent hours thinking about it all and had come to the conclusion that Hamish Grant had shown her the room as it had been on that night and if she returned, he would show her what had happened.

The argument continued but neither girl would change her mind. Sarah realised she could not sway her cousin, and she would have to go on her own. She got her bike out of the shed and prepared to leave.

"I'm warning you," Alison shouted. "I mean it. I really am telling Mum as soon as she gets home."

Sarah rode off down to the village leaving Alison in tears. She had worked out that she would be able to contrive more time alone in the tower room if she went on the last tour before the castle closed. So she sat on the shore of the loch thinking and absent-mindedly throwing pebbles into the water until her watch said three-thirty.

She parked her bike by the castle gate and went in. An elderly man sat at a small table in the entrance hall, issuing tickets for the next tour. The hall was already quite full of visitors waiting for the guide, and Sarah had little difficulty in making herself inconspicuous at the back of the crowd. She did not want to be recognised by Mrs Forbes, who might just be tempted to keep an eye on her after the incident of the candlestick.

"I should have disguised myself," she thought belatedly. "I'll just have to keep my head down and hope for the best."

Mrs Forbes appeared at the back of the hall, having steered the previous tourists into the gift shop as their only way out of the castle. She cleared her throat loudly and started her well-worn introduction.

"Craig Dubh Castle is named after the outcrop of black basalt rock on which it stands," she intoned. "In the Gaelic language, craig means rock and dubh means dark or black so you see that the name in English is Black Rock Castle. The Castle has been the home of the Grants of Glenmore for over four hundred years until the mysterious disappearance of the last laird in World War Two. The Grants of Glenmore are a remote offshoot of the mighty Clan Grant. It is believed that, originally, an impoverished younger son of the family hired himself as a mercenary to a Highland chieftain, who held the land around Loch More, and was given the chieftain's only daughter in marriage in recognition of his prowess in the wars between the clans. The chieftain's sons all died in battle and so the castle and lands became the property of the daughter and thus her husband."

Mrs Forbes moved towards the oak door leading from the left of the hall, obediently followed by the shuffling crowd of visitors.

"The castle consists of two main parts," she continued, pausing by the door, "the newer part, dating from the late eighteenth century, contains the domestic quarters and the family dining room, a small withdrawing room for the ladies and the large drawing room, which all contain their original furniture. The older part of the castle consists of the original tower house. It contains the armoury on the ground floor and the private apartments of the family on the two floors above. If you will all follow me now, we shall see this part first and return to the newer part of the house afterwards. I have to warn you that the spiral staircase is very steep and slippery so please take great care as we go up."

The guide led her party along the passage and into a large stone-flagged room at the bottom of the tower. The walls of the room were covered with old swords, muskets and pistols arranged into intricate patterns, separated by crossed pikes and flags. In glass cases were fine antique sporting guns, used by members of the family in previous centuries, and the military decorations won by previous generations of Grants. In one case there was a faded picture of a little boy holding up a medal.

Sarah read the label. 'Hamish Grant, aged 5 years, receiving his father's Victoria Cross, awarded for valour in the Great War when he was killed in action while rescuing injured members of his Company under fire. 1918.'

The famous bronze cross with the purple ribbon lay in the case next to the picture, and Sarah felt hot tears start in her eyes when she looked at the sad, lost, little face of the fatherless boy. How cruel it was, she thought, that the whole family should have completely died out after so many hundreds of years and even more so that the last of them almost certainly died in a violent and terrible way.

After the visitors had had a few minutes to wander around the armoury, Mrs Forbes called them together and led them up the spiral staircase to the next floor. She kept up her running commentary as the people cautiously mounted the steep stone stairs and she began to describe the family portraits on the walls of the passage.

Sarah kept right at the back but mingled with the last few people because the guide had a habit of checking that the last person in the crowd had caught up. She was not really listening to the guide's voice but was concentrating on remaining unseen. Once she started to climb the familiar stairs, she was conscious of a growing feeling of nervousness and she wished that Alison was with her. She didn't really feel afraid but she felt butterflies in her stomach and a little shivery feeling on her skin.

Mrs Forbes led the tour through the rooms on the first floor. Finally, she took the party up the last flight of stairs to the laird's room. At the top of the stairs, she stopped.

"I wonder if anyone knows what this is," she asked, as she drew back a tapestry curtain to reveal a tiny room built into the wall of the tower. The visitors shuffled obediently forward and peered in. Sarah, her face lowered, kept to the back of the crowd. The little alcove was empty except for a sort of stone bench, with a large round hole in the middle, against the outer wall.

"It looks like an old fashioned toilet," said a small, middle-aged man near the front.

Mrs Forbes gave him a patronising smile. "You're quite right. This is what is known as a garderobe, which was a polite word for an indoor privy. When the castle was built, the owner lived here on the top floor of the tower and had his own privy so that he would not have to climb up and down the spiral staircase in the middle of the night. We think it originally had a wooden seat with a smaller hole, which would have made it a little more comfortable on a cold winter's night."

"Where did the servants and the other people in the castle go, then?" a woman asked.

Mrs Forbes raised her chin slightly, as if the better to see her over the others' heads. "Ah," she said, "they would have had to go to latrines in the corner of the courtyard. The latrines were just deep holes in the ground with a seat and they must have been very unpleasant to use."

A thin American woman with pink glasses leaned forward slightly and sniffed disdainfully. "I guess this one don't smell too fresh, either."

Mrs Forbes gave her a slightly chilly smile. "Oh, I think not dear. You see the hole leads right down through the wall of the tower and we think it actually goes into a small cave, which is washed out by the tide twice a day. I suppose you could say it was one of the first flushing toilets." She laughed at her little joke and the visitors all smiled dutifully.

"She says that every time," Sarah said to herself, fidgeting with impatience.

"How do they know?" a girl asked.

Mrs Forbes raised her head again and said without a smile, "I expect somebody once went down there and looked, dear."

The girl giggled and a boy near Sarah made a disgusting noise and pushed his brother.

Mrs Forbes looked as though all this talk of toilets was quite enough. "Now, if you will all follow me, we will see the laird's private bedchamber."

"We seen his toilet so now we're seein' his chamber as well," said a fat-faced man in shirt sleeves and red braces. "You can't say we're not getting our money's worth on this trip." He grinned around at the other visitors as if expecting applause. His wife punched his arm and hissed at him to shut up.

Mrs Forbes pretended not to hear but her face had assumed a severe expression, with her lips pressed into a thin line. She paused outside an oak door with iron studs and turned to face the people as they straggled along the passage. She stood silently until they had all caught up. Some of them were still making jokes about toilets and visiting latrines in the winter, and the two boys were tapping and pushing each other and bumping into everybody.

The guide waited with a stony look on her face, like a schoolteacher with an unruly class, until she had embarrassed them into silence. Hiding at the back of the crowd, Sarah could have screamed with the awful tension of waiting while Mrs

Forbes went into her account of the mysterious disappearance of Hamish Grant.

"This is the laird's private bedroom," she said with a hard look at the man in braces. "This room was occupied by the lairds of Craig Dubh Castle for over four hundred years until nineteen forty. The last laird, Hamish Grant, disappeared from the castle on the night of June the fifteenth, nineteen forty and was never seen again. His Naval Officer's uniform was discovered in the sea-loch about a month later but his body was never found. After he disappeared, his wife refused to spend another night in this room. It has been left exactly as it was on the night Hamish Grant disappeared, and in the years since, many people have claimed that it is haunted."

"What do they think happened to him, then?" asked a tall thin boy with glasses.

"If they knew that, it wouldn't be a mystery would it?" his father muttered.

"Well, there were many rumours going round at the time," said Mrs Forbes. "Some people claimed he was really a German spy who had used his position in the Navy to pass on secret information to the enemy and when he was in danger of being unmasked he was picked up by a German submarine in the sea-loch in the dead of night. They think he threw his British uniform into the sea. Most of the local people thought he was far too fine a gentleman to betray his country. There were men from the Navy here investigating as well as the police. They didn't seem to find any clues and eventually they all left."

There was a buzz of interested comment among the visitors as they followed the guide into the room. Sarah waited until she was the last and then, turning swiftly, she ran back to the garderobe. Without drawing the curtain back, she lifted one edge and slipped inside the little alcove. She waited, hardly daring to breathe. It was her only chance. If she was discovered now, they would never let her near the place again.

It seemed like an age before she heard the door of the laird's room open again and Mrs Forbes shepherding her flock down the spiral staircase to visit the other part of the castle. Sarah stood with her body rigid, sure that the people who brushed by the other side of the curtain would hear her heart beating. Once, she saw tiny fingers grasp the edge of the curtain and glimpsed a little girl about to peer in when, in the nick of time, a woman's hand unceremoniously yanked the child away.

She waited until the noise of footsteps had died away before emerging from her hiding place. Slowly, she walked along the passageway to the oak door. Her heart was thumping beneath her ribs and she had a sick feeling in her stomach as she slowly pushed it open.

The room was exactly as she had last seen it. There was the massive four- poster bed still covered by the old tapestry bedcover with no sign of the dreadful brown stain. The enormous iron-bound chest stood against the left-hand wall, with the lid raised to reveal the jigsaw of black iron locks beneath.

Sarah went towards the huge stone fireplace and looked up at the portrait. She saw the sea-loch and the castle in the background, and then slowly she raised her eyes until she was looking into the face of Hamish Grant.

As she stood before the portrait, the painted blue eyes seemed to take on life. She became aware of them looking right into her, which created a prickling feeling as the small hairs rose on her skin. The rest of the room seemed to recede as if she were looking down a long tunnel. The young man's face seemed to grow until it filled the whole of her vision and once again she could hear a voice, as if from inside her own head, say,

"Help me, Sarah, help me."

She heard her own voice answer, "I am here, how can I help you?"

Suddenly, it was as if she were on the other side of the room. There was a glowing peat fire in the huge iron basket. In front of the fireplace was a young woman speaking angrily, clenching her fists and stamping her foot to emphasise her words. She was shouting at a young man, dressed in pyjamas, who stood with his back to her, folding clothes and placing them into a suitcase which lay next to a Naval Officer's uniform on the bed. From time to time, the man shook his head, as if refusing something, which only seemed to enrage the young woman more. She leaned forward and screamed something at the young man's back. He turned his head, said something curtly and returned to his packing.

A look of venomous rage twisted the woman's beautiful face into a vicious mask. Looking round her, she reached out for the heavy pewter candlestick on the mantelpiece. Grasping it with both hands, she crossed the room in two strides and brought it crashing down upon the back of the man's head. The young man pitched forward onto the bed with his arms outspread. His fingers grasped at the tapestry and dragged the bedcover with him as he slid down onto the floor. As he lay slumped against the side of the bed, blood poured from his injured head and made a dreadful spreading brown stain on the bedcover.

As the scene before her slowly faded, Sarah stood numb with shock for a long time, then, suddenly, she heard footsteps in the corridor outside the room. The footsteps stopped and she heard Mrs Forbes make an exclamation of annoyance as she spotted an empty crisp bag on the floor.

Sarah looked wildly around her. Seeing the open chest, she darted across to it and climbed in. She lowered the huge lid carefully and, hardly daring to breath, squinted through the crack beneath the edge of the lid. She saw the heavy oak door open and the sensible lovat-green tweed of Mrs Forbes' skirt appeared. There was a pause as the guide looked around the room and then with a click of the light switch, the skirt disappeared as the door closed.

Sarah lay still for as long as she could to make sure the guide had gone. When she was quite certain all was quiet, she stretched her cramped legs and flexed her shoulders. As she did so, her upper arm caught on one of the black iron levers and there was a loud thump as all the huge locks shot home!

***

Old Mr McGregor, who issued the tickets, let himself out of the castle through the little door set into the main gate. He exclaimed to himself as he saw the bicycle. Obviously, some careless young person had left it behind. Conscientiously, he wheeled it out of sight around the corner, to keep it safe until the owner returned to claim it.

Chapter 7

Jean Frazer turned her car off the main road and into the lane leading to her cottage. She had had a difficult afternoon. What a waste of time, she thought; all that arguing about petty details with silly pompous people with an inflated sense of their own importance.

"They only do it because it gives them a feeling of power and the opportunity to make a nuisance of themselves," she said aloud.

Jean put the frustrations of the afternoon out of her mind and sighed as she wondered what on earth to cook for dinner. Slowing down, she indicated right and turned into her driveway. Hardly had the car come to a halt when Alison came running down the path and pulled open the driver's door.

"Oh, Mum, oh Mum, where've you been? Something terrible's happened," she shrieked, hopping from one foot to the other and flapping her hands hysterically.

Jean's stomach gave a sickening lurch. "What is it?" she said in panic. "Has something happened to Daddy?" She lived in fear of something happening to her husband, Stewart, a geologist prospecting for oil in the dangerous waters of the North Sea.

Alison stopped still for a second, taken aback by the unexpected question, then she resumed her agitated dance. "No, no," she shouted, flapping and jigging frantically. "Sarah's gone, and I can't find her, and you didn't come home, and it's all my fault because I wouldn't go with her and now she's disappeared, and it's all my fault."

Jean stood up, grasped her daughter by the shoulders and shook her hard. "Stop it. Stop this and tell me properly. What's been going on and where's Sarah?"

"She's disappeared and I tried to stop her but I couldn't and I've looked everywhere and I know something dreadful has happened to her," Alison gabbled, beginning to jig up and down again.

Jean shook her roughly again and shouted at her. "Stop gabbling at me and stand still. Tell me properly what on earth you're talking about or I'll slap you!"

Alison burst into tears and started to tell her mother the whole story. Wringing her hands in misery, she told Jean how Sarah seemed obsessed by the conviction that Hamish Grant was asking her for help, about their visits to Constable Jamieson and Annie Logan and about Sarah's determination to return to the castle. She told her mother about seeing Sarah sleep-walking, and how she had refused to go with her to the castle, which caused the quarrel between them, and about Sarah going off on her own.

"Oh, I do wish you'd told me all this before. What time did she go?"

"She went on her bike about half-past two," Alison replied wretchedly. "I knew the castle closed at half-past four and when she hadn't come back by five o'clock I went to look for her but the castle was closed and her bike wasn't there. I looked everywhere for her but I couldn't find her and you didn't come home." She burst into loud sobs again,

"Get in the car and we'll go and look for her," said Jean firmly. "She's probably gone off somewhere on her bike. I'll give her a piece of my mind when I get hold of her."

Jean reversed out of the drive and drove down the hill back to the main road. Although she had used a firm and exasperated voice for Alison's benefit, she could not erase from her mind the vision of the white clad girl standing in a trance by the window, staring at the black bulk of the castle silhouetted against the moonlit water. She couldn't forget how she had felt that her niece's reaction to the castle and its mystery was more than the natural response of an impressionable girl, and that she had had a sense of unease bordering on fear about it.

She drove rapidly round the bay; in a few minutes they had reached the castle and she swung the car into the parking area. She hurried across the causeway to the great wooden gate but it was firmly locked, as was the little door set in it. She banged on the door hopefully and then stood back, looking up at the castle as if expecting to see a light or signs of movement. Turning, she hurried back to the car. She drove quickly back towards the village. About half-way down the straggling main street, she stopped the car outside the grey stone house belonging to Mrs Forbes.

Jean opened the green painted wicket gate, walked up the brick path to the green front door and banged the heavy brass knocker rather harder than she had intended. After a few moments, Mrs Forbes opened the door and stood looking at her with an air of surprise.

"Good evening, Mrs Frazer," she boomed in her penetrating voice. "It is not often that I have the pleasure of a visit from you." She smiled an insincere, mechanical smile at Jean but did not invite her in.

"Good evening, Mrs Forbes," Jean began. "I'm sorry to bother you at home but I'm trying to find my niece Sarah and I was hoping you could help."

"I cannot think how I could be of help to you in that, Mrs Frazer," Mrs Forbes replied, raising her eyebrows in affected astonishment.

"We know she visited the castle this afternoon but she hasn't returned home and I was hoping someone may have seen where she went or if she left with anyone."

"Oh, no my dear, you are quite mistaken. Your niece was not at the castle this afternoon."

"But she definitely intended to go when she left home," Jean insisted. "Are you quite sure you didn't see her?"

Mrs Forbes pursed her lips. "Oh, quite sure. When your daughter and your niece visited the castle last week, the careless

girl nearly damaged a valuable old candlestick; I would have kept a very close eye on her had she come again today, or any other day, I can assure you. I am afraid you will have to look elsewhere." With that, she smiled her false smile again and closed the door.

Jean walked slowly back to the car, completely baffled. It didn't make sense, she wouldn't make huge scenes about going back to the castle, storm off on her own and then not go there after all, surely? The possibility that Sarah had been abducted on her way to the castle entered her mind and she began to feel panicky. Getting into the car she told Alison what Mrs Forbes had said.

"Oh, but that's stupid," said Alison wildly. "She must have gone, I know she did. That horrible old woman is telling lies."

"Don't be silly. Why would she tell lies, for heaven's sake? Let's go home and see if she's come back while we've been gone."

She turned the car round and drove back to the cottage. Jean stayed in the driver's seat with the engine running while Alison jumped out and ran up to the house calling for Sarah. She went inside and rushed from room to room calling her name but there was no reply.

Alison ran back to the car looking wretched. "She's not there, Mum," about to cry again.

"We'll just have to drive round until we find her, then."

Jean reversed out of the drive again. She drove down to the main road, through the village and out towards Glenmore. It was a dull and overcast evening and there was no one about. After about four miles she turned the car around and drove back through the village and out along the road to Fort William. Passing the castle, she stopped and looked searchingly but there was no sign of life and she drove on. Eventually, following a forlorn hope, she arrived at Annie Logan's cottage at Coinach.

The couple were seated at the kitchen table eating their evening meal when she knocked. Annie answered the door and Jean hurriedly explained that she was looking for Sarah. Sitting in the car, Alison saw the kindly woman shake her head with a worried look and she felt the tears start to fill her eyes again. Jean said her thanks and apologies and hurried down the path to the car. Annie remained standing at the cottage door until they had turned round and driven off.

"There goes that idea. I suppose it was stupid of me to hope that she had gone there again but I just don't know where to look now."

"Oh Mum, I'm so frightened," Alison whispered. "Where can she be? She must have gone to the castle, I know she must."

Jean drove back to Kilmore far too fast for the narrow road but she was now really afraid.

"When I get my hands on her, she won't sit down for a week," she said for Alison's benefit.

Over the pass, Jean drove as fast as she dared down the hairpin bends to the loch shore. As they passed the castle, they both turned and stared at the brooding mass of stone but she drove on, as fast as she could.

***

In the darkened tower room, Sarah had struggled to open the huge lid of the chest when she had heard the iron locks thump closed. She pushed and kicked in blind panic, whimpering in fear, but, lying on her side in the confined space, she could not exert any real force. It would not have helped her if she could, because the chest had been made massive to resist attempts to open it by force. Her sleeve was caught in the iron lock mechanism so she could not turn over, or properly move her left arm to push. As her feeble struggles failed to move the lid of the chest, she felt terror and panic rise in her. She screamed a terrible scream of pure fear, over and over again until, finally, she fainted.

After some time, she recovered consciousness and for a second she did not remember where she was but was only aware that it was dark and that something seemed to have hold of her. As the awful realisation of her situation returned, she began wailing fearfully and started to struggle feebly again. The muscles of her legs suddenly contracted with cramp and she shouted with the pain and tried unsuccessfully to straighten them. Her hands were hurting where she had hit in panic at the sides of the chest with her fists. For a moment the pain seemed to calm her thoughts. She struggled to push her right arm upwards from beneath her body in an attempt to grasp hold of one of the lock levers. With a tremendous effort, she managed to feel the shape of one of the iron bars with her fingers but she could not exert any pressure upon it. She tried to tear the trapped material of her sleeve by pulling at it but the nylon of her anorak was too strong. She twisted her left hand as far as she could until she could feel it touch her right hand and she was able to half grasp the iron lever. She pushed and pulled with her fingers to no avail and felt the panic rising in her again. It was getting very hot and hard to breathe in the chest.

"I'm going to suffocate! Please help me! Somebody, please help me! Daddy, please come and help me!" she screamed again and again.

Chapter 8

Jean pulled up outside the Police House with a squeal of brakes and the noise of locked wheels sliding on the gravel. She was relieved to see the van outside and ran up to the front door with Alison. Entering the bare porch, she rang the bell urgently. Sergeant Campbell slid open the hatch immediately and, seeing the expression on Jean's face, he reached across and opened the blue door before she could speak.

"What is it, Mrs Frazer?" he said sharply as he stood framed in the doorway. Jean started to pour out her story as he ushered them both into the living room.

"Some tea, Maggie," he said to his wife, who had been looking on with concern, "and put a dram in Mrs Frazer's." He gently pushed Jean and Alison down onto the sofa.

"Go on, lassie," he said to Jean. "Tell me the whole story as quickly as you can without leaving anything out."

Mother and daughter told the sergeant about the events leading up to Sarah's disappearance. He listened gravely, watching their faces with his searching look and occasionally interrupting with a question.

"So, Mrs Forbes is quite certain Sarah didn't go there this afternoon?"

Jean sipped at her tea and coughed as the whisky in it caught at her throat. "She says she would have remembered her because of the incident with the candlestick," she answered miserably.

The sergeant frowned in thought. "There's one other person who might remember her," he said suddenly. "Old Alistair McGregor takes the money at the door. If you and your daughter would like to come with me now, I think we should go and see him first." They hurried out of the Police House.

"Would you mind if we use your car, Mrs Frazer?" Sergeant Campbell asked, "we won't all fit in the van."

Jean drove the short distance to Mr McGregor's cottage at well above the speed limit. The sergeant said nothing. He crossed the pavement in two strides and knocked on the faded blue door. After what seemed an interminable time, they heard the bolt being pulled back and the door opened a few inches. When he saw the sergeant's familiar uniform, the old man opened the door wide and looked questioningly at the unexpected group.

"May we come in for a wee word about an urgent matter, Alistair?" the sergeant said gently.

"What's this all about, then?" Mr McGregor looked from one to the other. "I haven't had a run in with the *polis* for quite a time. Is it my TV licence you're after, then, or the whisky I make in the woodshed?"

Smiling at the old man's joke, Sergeant Campbell rapidly explained why they had come. "Do you think you saw this young lassie, then, Alistair?"

The old man shook his head doubtfully. "Well, it's hard to say," he answered slowly. Then, with a wicked grin, "Is she pretty? I usually remember the pretty ones. You might say it's the only hobby an old man has left." He gestured with a gnarled hand. "Haven't you got one of they picture things? You know, they identikits, that would maybe bring her to mind."

Sergeant Campbell shook his head, struggling to control his impatience.

Jean thought she would scream if this took any longer.

"I've got a picture," Alison volunteered, to everyone's surprise. She held out the locket which she wore on a thin gold chain around her neck. Inside was a tiny photograph of Sarah.

"Will you just have a look at the wee picture?" the sergeant asked.

The old man peered at the proffered locket. "I'll just have to get my right glasses," he mumbled, looking around him vaguely. He went indecisively from the table to the chair and then over to the bookcase muttering.

Jean fought desperately to control her desire to scream at him.

"Aye, aye," he said to himself as a thought occurred to him and he disappeared into the kitchen.

Jean tugged the sergeant's arm. "Oh please hurry," she said, "we're wasting time."

Sergeant Campbell looked grim. "Aye, I'm afraid this was a mistake."

Just then the old man returned clutching his reading glasses case. With painful slowness he exchanged them for the pair he had on and carefully placed the others in the case.

"I don't want to hurry you, Alistair," the sergeant prompted gently, "but we must get on and find the lassie."

Mr McGregor peered at the tiny picture.

Jean clenched her hands until the nails dug into her palms.

"Oh, yes," he said, "I mind that lassie well."

The others straightened up and smiled at each other with relief.

"The poor wee thing was taken poorly one day last week."

"Oh, my God no!" Jean gasped in dismay. "I thought he meant…"

Sergeant Campbell grasped her arm and said carefully to the old man, "Today, Alistair. Did you see the lassie at the castle today?"

"That's what I just said," the old man retorted, indignantly. "I mind her because she was the same one who was ill last week."

Jean could hardly bear the rush of relief which flooded into her. "Did you see her leave afterwards?" she asked urgently.

The old man smiled. "Oh, no. The folk don't come out past me in the hall; they have to go through the gift shop, to get some more money out of them."

Sergeant Campbell hastily thanked Mr McGregor and made for the door. Without asking he climbed into the driving seat of Jean's car and with a roar and a spurt of gravel, accelerated down the main street of the village. They screeched to a halt outside Mrs Forbes' house.

"Stay in the car please, Mrs Frazer," he ordered. He ran up the path and banged on the green door.

Mrs Forbes opened her front door and glared at the policeman. Her glance took in the car and the faces of Jean and Alison watching anxiously and she pursed her lips and frowned. "Kindly do not hammer on my door in that fashion, Sergeant," she demanded, icily.

Sergeant Campbell ignored her remark. "I am engaged in an urgent enquiry, Mrs Forbes, and I think you can be of assistance," he said in a hard voice.

"Do not take that tone with me, Sergeant," she replied indignantly. "I have already told Mrs Frazer I have not set eyes on her wretched niece."

"I understand you've already said that the girl did not visit the castle today but I have just now come from Alistair McGregor, who remembers selling her a ticket," he answered firmly.

"Oh, rubbish. That silly old fool doesn't know what day it is," she answered rudely. "I can assure you, that girl did not tour the castle or I should have watched her very carefully. In my opinion, she is a bad lot that one. She has probably run away to Glasgow to become one of those hippies. If you ask me, you would do better to start looking there. Now, if you will excuse me, I cannot help you any more."

With that she started to close the door but the sergeant's foot got there first. "I'm sorry you are being inconvenienced, but I wish to search the castle to satisfy myself the missing girl is not there."

"That is quite unnecessary," Mrs Forbes replied venomously. "I always check every room after closing time to make sure everyone has gone. There is no possibility that the girl could still be there."

"I'm afraid I must insist you accompany me to the castle while I look for myself."

Mrs Forbes drew herself up to her full height. "Are you suggesting I do not do my job conscientiously?" she boomed angrily.

"Not at all, but I still insist that you bring the keys and accompany me to the castle," he replied, fixing her with an unflinching stare.

Mrs Forbes held his gaze for a moment longer and looked as if she would continue to argue. Suddenly, she looked away. "Very well, it seems I have no choice, but I warn you, I intend to complain in the strongest possible terms to your superiors."

"Aye, well, you do that, but I would be obliged if you would get the keys and come with me as fast as you can," Sergeant Campbell replied, still holding open the door with his foot.

After a few moments, Mrs Forbes emerged from her house wearing her topcoat and carrying a large bunch of keys in her hand. The sergeant held open the rear door of Jean's car and she got in beside Alison. She sat in silent fury until they reached the castle and, without a word, she got out of the car and stalked off over the causeway.

Sergeant Campbell went round to the front of the car and pulled up the metal post set into a hole at the end of the causeway, put there to stop the tourists driving their cars up to the castle. He slid back into his seat and drove over the causeway as far as the great wooden gate where Mrs Forbes was sorting through her bunch of keys.

They tried to contain their impatience while the woman unlocked the little door and led them across the courtyard to the main entrance. It was now nearly dark, due in part to the heavy cloud and drizzle, and Alison, looking up at the grim walls around her, clung to her mother's arm. Jean was in a ferment of impatience at the guide's ponderous progress. She didn't think there was any possibility of Sarah's still being in the castle. Perhaps she has run away, she thought. Young girls do such silly things on the spur of the moment, it was certainly not beyond the bounds of possibility.

In the entrance hall, Sergeant Campbell turned to Jean and Alison. "I would prefer you to remain here if you wouldn't mind, Mrs Frazer."

Jean opened her mouth to object but the sergeant's direct stare flicked to Alison and then back to her and she understood. Nodding silently, she pulled Alison towards an oak settle by the wall and sat down, silencing the girl's protests.

The sergeant turned to Mrs Forbes. "We'll do the inside of the house first, then if we draw a blank we'll search the stables and the gatehouse."

They began in the old wine cellars and worked their way upwards through the kitchens and the servant's quarters. There proved to be a surprising number of cupboards and other places where a person could hide, or be hidden, thought the sergeant grimly, and their progress was slow. Eventually, they completed their search of the newer part of the house and emerged into the hall again. Jean and Alison half rose but the sergeant shook his head.

Turning to Mrs Forbes, who was still silently fuming, he said, "The lassie was fascinated by the mystery. She thought she'd seen a ghost in the tower room. I think we should have looked there first and worked our way down."

Mrs Forbes sighed in exasperation, "I assure you, I checked that room as well as the others and there was no one there. You are just wasting your time."

The sergeant didn't reply but was inclined to agree. Taking her elbow, he propelled her firmly towards the spiral staircase. They went through the armoury and up the steep stone stairs, switching on the lights as they went.

At the top, the sergeant pulled back the curtain of the garderobe and glanced inside. "Not much room for anything there," he muttered.

They continued along the passage to the iron-studded oak door of the tower room. Mrs Forbes fiddled with her bunch of keys, selected the right one and turned the huge old lock. She swung open the door and clicked on the light. Sergeant Campbell walked a few paces into the room and looked around. He went across to the massive bed and knelt down to peer underneath but under the drapes it was solid panelling.

"As you can see Sergeant, there is no one here, as I told you."

He put his hand on the bed and stood up. As he did so, he heard Mrs Forbes make a sound of annoyance and turned to look at her as she walked quickly over to the chest.

"Who has interfered with this? The lid should be open against the wall." She attempted to lift the heavy lid and stood back puzzled. "Why, it's locked," she said in astonishment. "Who could have done that? I am the only one with a key."

Sergeant Campbell crossed the room in two strides. "Quickly woman, the key," he demanded urgently, holding out his hand.

"It's no use," said Mrs Forbes holding on to it. "There are six locks which must be opened in the right order or it will not open."

"Then do it quickly," he ordered. "There may be no time to lose."

He watched with impatience as she slowly fumbled with the locks. First one side and then the other in no obvious sequence. He counted five locks but she seemed to be struggling with the last.

"Quick as you can, please," he urged.

"I can't understand it; it seems to be stuck."

"Please, let me." He pushed her aside. Grasping the massive iron key in both hands, he twisted hard. For a moment nothing happened, then the key turned and the six locks shot back with a loud thump. Mrs Forbes bent to lift the lid. The sergeant quickly grabbed her arm and moved her back from the chest. Bracing himself, he raised the lid.

Inside, they saw the body of the missing girl, lying curled up on her side. The sergeant swore under his breath and swiftly knelt down. As he reached for Sarah's wrist to check her pulse, she whimpered slightly and opened her eyes.

Chapter 9

Sergeant Campbell felt a rush of relief when he realised Sarah was alive. Lifting the semi-conscious girl in his arms, he carried her carefully down the spiral staircase to her frantic aunt and cousin in the hall. He laid her on the oak settle and Jean knelt beside her, crushing her with a desperate hug of relief. Sarah clung to her aunt's neck, sobbing uncontrollably, while Alison, the tears streaming down her face, patted and stroked the bits of her cousin she could reach.

The sergeant quickly checked Sarah for obvious injuries. "She seems all right. I think we should get her home as quickly as we can and then let the doctor have a proper look at her."

He gathered Sarah up in his arms again and carried her out of the door and across the courtyard. They had some trouble negotiating the little door in the gate, then he placed her on the back seat of the car with her head on Jean's lap. He directed Alison to the front passenger seat and turned to Mrs Forbes, who had been following silently, a few paces behind.

"I expect you'd like to lock up now, Mrs Forbes. I'm very grateful for your kind assistance." With that he slid into the driver's seat and started the engine.

"But how am I expected to get home, Sergeant?" she protested indignantly, holding on to the door handle.

Sergeant Campbell smiled cheerfully at her. "Sorry, can't stop, we must get the lassie home to her bed and the doctor.

I'm sure you understand. Thank you again for your cooperation and goodnight." He pulled the door firmly closed and putting the car in gear, reversed rapidly over the causeway, leaving Mrs Forbes speechless with fury.

***

The doctor carefully examined Sarah and after pronouncing that all was well, he took Jean on one side.

"I'm going to give her a couple of fairly strong sleeping tablets before I go. I want her to get a good night's sleep. I can't tell if she'll suffer any after-effects; we'll just have to wait and see."

"What after-effects have you in mind?" Jean asked anxiously.

"Well, in the short term, I wouldn't be at all surprised if she had nightmares about her ordeal. In the long term, it's possible she may develop a fear of confined spaces. We'll have to face that if and when it arises."

After promising to call in the next day, he left a little while later with Sergeant Campbell.

***

The room was filled with sunshine as Sarah slowly opened her eyes. She was lying in her own bed and as she looked about, she saw the familiar sloping ceiling and the pretty curtains, with the little pink rosebuds. As the events of yesterday began to come back to her, it all seemed unreal, a bad dream, but gradually her memory began to clear and she shivered as she realised what had happened was only too real.

The door opened and Jean entered with a tray. When she saw Sarah was awake, she hurriedly put the tray on the dressing table and, sinking to her knees at the bedside, enfolded her in her arms and hugged her so hard that Sarah could hardly breathe. Jean kissed Sarah's cheeks and forehead, then rested the girl's head on her shoulder and stroked her hair, smiling down at her.

"You naughty girl, you frightened us all half to death."

Sarah snuggled closer to her aunt. "Oh, Auntie Jean," hot tears starting in her eyes. "I was so frightened, I thought I was going to die."

"You nearly did, my precious," Jean said with a lump in her throat and close to tears herself. "Please! Don't ever, ever, do anything like that again."

Sarah buried her face into Jean's shoulder and whispered, "Oh, I'm so sorry. I didn't mean to cause you any worry; it just sort of happened."

Jean raised Sarah's head and searched her face. "But what on earth made you get into the chest in the first place?"

"I heard Mrs Forbes coming and I didn't want her to catch me, so I hid in the chest but then it locked itself and I couldn't get out." Sarah shivered violently at the memory.

"Yes, but why did you go there at all?" asked Jean, ducking her head slightly and searching Sarah's face.

Sarah hung her head. "You'll think I'm stupid, but I thought Hamish Grant would show me what happened to him on the night he disappeared."

Jean tightened her lips and looked stern. "Well, this is as good a time as any to make one thing quite clear. You have got to forget all this rubbish about Hamish Grant and the mystery, and I mean right now. After last night I will not hear one more word about it in this house. I don't want to hear even mention of the name. I want you to promise me, here and now, you'll forget the whole thing."

"But, Aunt Jean," Sarah began, intending to tell her what she had seen in the tower room.

"But nothing!" Jean interrupted sharply. "You promise me now or I will send you home today. I phoned your father in New York last night and he wanted to come straight back and take you home. I told him you were safe and unharmed and he should stay on and finish his work but if you don't promise to forget about Hamish Grant, I'll telephone Mrs Jones and put you on the train home tonight."

"Oh! please don't, Auntie Jean," Sarah pleaded, appalled at the thought of spending the rest of the summer holiday with her father's elderly housekeeper. "I will promise. Whatever you say. Let me stay here with you and Alison."

"All right, but just remember, break your promise and it's the next train home. I mean it; make no mistake."

"I shan't break my promise. Oh! thanks for not sending me back." She hugged her aunt gratefully.

Jean smiled down at the anxious young face. "Well, let's say no more about it. She rose to her feet and went over to the dressing table for the tray. "Now then, I've brought you your favourite breakfast." She set it down on Sarah's knees. "Two boiled eggs and toast soldiers. Make sure you eat it."

Sarah picked up a buttered toast soldier, wincing as she attempted to bend her swollen knuckles. At that moment the door opened slightly and the top of Alison's blonde head above two curious eyes appeared round the edge. When she saw Sarah sitting up in bed, she flung open the door, charged across the room and with loud shrieks of exaggerated joy flung herself dramatically across her cousin. Jean deftly fielded the breakfast tray as it was sliding to the floor.

Yanking Alison off the bed, she replaced the tray. "Get off her, you silly ass, I want Sarah to eat her breakfast. Just act a bit more sensibly, please."

Jean left the two girls together, Sarah sitting up in bed, painfully dipping soldiers into her boiled egg, while Alison perched on the edge grinning inanely at her.

She examined the grazed knuckles. "I bet those are sore." Then, with a wicked smile. "You're going to find some things difficult to do for a bit, aren't you?" She rocked back and forth with laughter at her own disgusting thoughts.

"I'll make you do it for me, then," Sarah replied quickly.

Both girls shrieked with laughter at the thought. On the landing, outside the door, Jean heard the hilarity and tutted, smiling to herself.

Alison heard her mother go downstairs. "Tell me what happened at the castle," she urged.

Sarah stopped smiling and looked anxious. "I can't. I promised your Mum not to talk about it any more; or she'll send me home."

"She doesn't mean it, anyway it's all right, she can't hear. I heard her go downstairs," Alison encouraged.

"No, I don't want to," Sarah answered, miserably. "You don't understand. She really does mean it and I don't want to have to live with Mrs Jones for weeks."

"Don't be a twit!" howled Alison indignantly, standing up. "You've got to tell me what happened."

Sarah looked at her in desperate anguish. "But I promised."

"But you can't not tell me, you mean pig," Alison shouted.

At that moment, the door opened and Jean entered with a cup of tea. She looked searchingly from her indignant daughter to her anxious niece, who was staring at her guiltily.

"Right, young lady," she said to Alison. "Out you go and get dressed, we'll have the doctor here any minute." She jerked her head at the open door and Alison swept out, pouting. Handing the tea to Sarah, Jean bent down and straightened the bedclothes.

"Stay here until we hear what the doctor has to say and then you can get up."

***

After the doctor had left, the two girls sat in the kitchen. Alison had her head resting on her forearms on the table and was silently sulking, while Jean brushed Sarah's long dark hair. They heard the sound of a car door closing and Jean went to the front door. There was the crunch of footsteps on the gravel, followed by Sergeant Campbell's cheerful voice.

He entered the kitchen with his cap under his arm and smiled down at Sarah. "I can't tell you how pleased I am to see you sitting there. You gave us all a nasty fright last night."

Sarah smiled timidly at the burly policeman as he accepted the chair offered by Jean.

"I'm really, really sorry, Mr Campbell. I honestly didn't mean to worry anybody."

"It was certainly a daft thing to do though."

Jean interrupted quickly. "I've made Sarah promise to forget about all that stupid business so I'd rather she didn't talk about it."

The sergeant turned towards her and looked at her levelly for a moment. "I understand how you feel, Mrs Frazer, but I have to put in a report. Unless the lassie is too ill to make a statement, which she clearly isn't, then I'm afraid she's going to have to answer some questions."

"But it will only upset her again, don't you see?" Jean retorted angrily. "I really don't see why you can't just treat the whole thing as an adolescent prank and let us forget it."

"I'm very sorry, Mrs Frazer," he insisted, "but you must realise that it's not up to me. I have to go by the book. You are, of course, welcome to be present all the time or even to have your solicitor present if you like but it really isn't necessary. The matter isn't that serious."

"Just what exactly is the situation, then?" Jean asked, still a little hostile.

"Well, the position, as I see it, is that the lassie was trespassing on private property," he began. "I've been to see Mrs Forbes first thing this morning and, as you might expect, she was demanding everything short of the death penalty but I was able to assure her that, as no damage was done, there has been no offence committed. Trespass, as I was pleased to point out to her, is only a civil offence, not a crime. I also just happened to mention that the lassie being on the premises when she was supposed to have checked there was no one left may possibly be taken by her employers as a sign of negligence on her part. I can tell you she was spitting nails after that but I think she'll keep quiet on the whole."

Despite herself, Jean laughed. "You're a born diplomat, Sergeant. You're wasted in the police, you ought to have joined the Foreign Office."

"Aye, I know," he replied, "I always thought I was in the wrong station in life, if you'll forgive the pun. Still, the fact is I have to put in a report about the incident, so are you agreeable to my asking the lassie some questions?"

Jean pulled a face and sighed. "I think we should ask the person most concerned." She turned towards Sarah, who had been following the conversation apprehensively. "Will it upset you to answer the sergeant's questions? Don't be afraid to say so if it will."

"You're not in any trouble with the law, lassie," the sergeant assured her. "I just have to know what happened for my report."

"No, it's all right, I don't mind, really I don't," Sarah answered quickly, looking anxiously from the sergeant to her aunt.

Jean lowered her eyes to the table and sighed. "Oh, all right then, let's get it over with."

Sergeant Campbell smiled gratefully and turned to Sarah. "Your aunt and Alison told me why you were interested in the castle," he began gently. "I know about the vision or the ghost or whatever it was, so don't be embarrassed. I just want you to tell me all about yesterday in your own words."

Alison sat up eagerly, all ears.

Sarah pouted defensively. "I suppose you think I'm just an hysterical little girl imagining things?"

The sergeant smiled at her flushed face. "Not at all. I believe there are things we don't always understand. In any case it doesn't matter what I think, does it? Just you tell me what happened and why."

Sarah smiled back at him, suddenly relieved. "I wanted to go back to the tower room on my own you see," she began. "I felt sure Hamish Grant was asking me for help and the more I thought about it, the more I was sure what I saw the first time we went to the castle was how the room had been on the night he disappeared and if I went again, he'd show me what happened."

"And did he?" Alison interrupted, wriggling with impatience.

Her mother shot her a steely glance and she subsided into her chair.

"Go on, lassie," Sergeant Campbell encouraged.

Sarah explained how she had avoided Mrs Forbes' eye during the tour and hidden in the garderobe so she could be in the tower room alone.

"When I went into the room, it all seemed normal at first until I looked at the picture again."

Alison wriggled impatiently in her chair. She leaned forward, her eyes shining, "I wish you'd get on with it."

Jean and the sergeant both glared at her this time, and she rolled her eyes upwards and pouted defiantly.

"What happened then?" Sergeant Campbell prompted gently.

"Well, I felt very funny again and suddenly it seemed like I was watching a film. I could see a man and a very pretty woman and they seemed to be arguing. She was shouting at him and he kept on ignoring her and packing his suitcase on the bed. Then he said something to her and turned his back and she grabbed the candlestick on the mantleshelf and hit him on the head with it. Then he sort of collapsed on the bed and then sank down onto the floor. There was blood all over the bedcover, just like I saw it the first time."

"See, I told you he was done in, didn't I," shouted Alison in excitement and was glared at again.

"No, you didn't! You said he'd fallen in the loch," Sarah shouted heatedly.

"Never mind who said what," the sergeant interrupted. "Let's get on. And you think it was Hamish Grant you saw?"

"Pretty bloody obvious, isn't it?" said Alison, scornfully.

Her mother rose to her feet and, grabbing her by the collar, hoisted her bodily from her chair and pushed her out of the kitchen.

Sergeant Campbell turned back to Sarah, suppressing a smile. "Go on, lassie."

"Well, I suppose it must have been; besides, his uniform was on the bed."

"He wasn't wearing it, then?"

"No, I should have told you. He was in his pyjamas, as if he was ready for bed."

Sergeant Campbell nodded. "What happened then?"

"The picture just disappeared and I heard Mrs Forbes coming."

"Tell us what you did next."

Sarah described how she had hidden in the chest and how

she had accidentally tripped the locks. When she recalled her terror at being trapped, she felt a sick feeling in her stomach but to her surprise, the memory of her ordeal was not as upsetting as it had been.

"I hope you realise what a close shave you had," he told her seriously. "You could've easily suffocated if we hadn't found you when we did."

"Oh, yes I do. Really I do," she said earnestly. "I won't do it again."

He chuckled, "You won't get the chance in that castle. Mrs Forbes will set the dogs on you if you go within a mile of the place."

Alison had been lurking outside the kitchen door muttering and could contain herself no longer. She poked her head into the room, ready to dodge her mother's hand.

"Aren't you going to arrest someone for murdering Hamish Grant?" she demanded.

Sergeant Campbell turned towards the door and said seriously, "I'm afraid a vision doesn't count as evidence in court, lassie."

"What will you put in your report?" Jean asked.

He smiled. "I shall report that a young girl stayed behind after the tour, hoping to see the ghost they tell the tourists about and that she was accidentally locked inside the antique chest she'd hidden in."

"But what about Hamish Grant?"

"I don't think my superiors would like me to report evidence given by a ghost," he said, smiling slightly. "I think I should find myself drawing my pension sooner than I'd thought."

"So nothing will be done about it?" Jean frowned.

"I didn't say that, did I?" he replied, enigmatically, as he rose to leave.

***

On his way back through the village, the sergeant saw Mrs Forbes sweeping her garden path. Stopping his van by the gate, he leaned over and opened the passenger window.

"I just thought you'd like to know the young lassie is fine and there's no harm done."

Mrs Forbes drew herself up and glared at the policeman's smiling face framed in the window. She snorted furiously and, without speaking, she turned and stamped into the house, slamming the front door behind her.

Sergeant Campbell put the van into gear and drove off down the street laughing.

Mrs Forbes stood in her hall, then, her mind made up, she reached for the telephone and dialled the number of the Glasgow Sunday Post.

Chapter 10

When the sergeant had gone, Jean decided they should go out to lunch as a special treat to help Sarah forget her ordeal. They piled into the car and set off down the hill. They drove through the village and around the shore of the loch to Glenmore. The road climbed steadily, following the course of the river up Glen More. After a mile or so the glen became much narrower. On the left was a steep drop through pine trees into the rocky bed of the river, whose peaty water foamed white as it gushed over jagged boulders or made long, still, tea-brown pools where small, golden, wild trout jumped. On the other side, the hillside rose steeply, clothed in the sombre pines of the forest, the dark barrier only broken by the occasional forestry track climbing up into the unknown.

The road followed the twists and turns of the river, the bends becoming ever tighter and steeper with raw, red rock faces showing where it had been blasted from the hillside. Each bend had to be approached cautiously, since it was impossible to see if there was anything coming from the opposite direction. A crash here could mean over the side and into the river, but fortunately there was not much traffic except for the odd forestry or hydro-electric company Land Rover and an occasional private car.

On a particularly steep bend, they came face to face with a giant, articulated timber-truck, loaded with huge logs, gingerly feeling its way round from the other direction. Jean stopped with a jerk. There was obviously no way past this monster. She had to reverse a considerable distance, hoping that nothing would appear behind her, until she could steer the car into a passing place. It was right on the apex of a bend and seemed to hang out over the edge of the slope with nothing but a flimsy-looking barrier between them and a long drop into the river.

They reached the summit and the hillsides opened out until they were running along a narrow valley. The road ran on between oak trees and huge Scots pines, beyond which were small fields of lush grass with black cattle contentedly grazing. Here the river was broad and shallow with gentle bends marked by banks of golden gravel. Occasionally they passed little groups of farm cottages, each hamlet with its bright red post box and telephone kiosk at the roadside. After about four miles, the main road turned sharply and crossed the river by an old stone bridge, while a smaller road, signposted 'Glen Beg', continued straight ahead. Just beyond the bridge was a small hamlet, dominated by a large stone-built hotel. Jean pulled off the road onto the gravel forecourt and they all trooped into the restaurant.

The hotel catered mainly for keen fishermen, who were not about to interrupt their pursuit of the elusive salmon to return for lunch, so, apart from two elderly German ladies sitting in a corner, they had the elegant dining room entirely to themselves. Sarah and Jean chose a poached-salmon open sandwich with prawn mayonnaise and salad but Alison announced she needed solid food to keep up her strength and ordered a sirloin steak sandwich and chips.

When it arrived, Sarah leaned over in an exaggerated inspection and said loudly, "That should do wonders for the size of your bum."

This observation provoked immediate violence from Alison and Jean had to intervene quickly before everything finished up on the floor.

"Behave yourselves, can't you?" she hissed at them as she pushed them back into their chairs. "You'll get us thrown out in a minute." She looked around sheepishly. Fortunately, the waitresses had disappeared into the kitchen but the two German ladies were staring at them in silent disapproval.

In spite of this unfortunate beginning, they enjoyed a splendid and leisurely lunch. The girls followed their main course with huge sickly-looking ice-cream sundaes and Jean had a vast slice of thick lemon meringue pie. In a mood of contented lethargy they finished off with coffee and mints.

Jean looked at her watch. "Do you realise it's nearly half-past two? If you two can move after what you've put away, I think we should get going. I really need to get some work done today or I won't finish the illustrations for the new book in time."

While Jean paid the bill, the girls strolled gently to the car.

Alison puffed out her cheeks and blew noisily. "Strewth, I can hardly move."

"That's because you're so bloated and fat," Sarah responded instantly.

Alison only managed the energy for a small punch on her arm.

The return journey didn't seem to take half as long. It seemed no time at all until they were descending the winding road above Glenmore. As they turned the last bend above the village, the whole of Loch More was laid out beneath them in a breathtakingly beautiful panorama, with the afternoon sun already getting lower over the distant islands to the west.

Sarah could clearly see the houses at Kilmore, although they were at least five miles away, and beyond the village the loch shore curved round the shallow bay to where Craig Dubh Castle stood on its rocks.

As she saw the castle in the distance, she felt a little shiver run over her skin and the little hairs prickled on the back of her neck. She stole a quick sidelong glance at the others to see if they had noticed her reaction but Jean was far too busy negotiating the steep road and Alison was busily occupied, painting her toe-nails red.

When they were passing Willie Jamieson's neat little cottage, none of them noticed the police van parked outside.

***

After dinner that evening, they were watching television. At about eight o'clock the telephone rang in the hall and Alison went to answer it. After a minute or so she burst into the room.

"Hey! You'll never guess what." She jigged up and down with delight. "There's a reporter on the phone from the Glasgow Sunday Post, and she wants to come and interview Sarah about the ghost and getting shut in the chest and everything." She squealed with exaggerated joy and tugged at Sarah's arm. "Quickly, come and talk to her, you're going to be famous. You'll probably be on television as well!"

Sarah started to get up hesitantly.

Jean rose quickly from her chair. "Hold it! Stay exactly where you are. You're certainly not talking to any reporters, so forget it. Just leave her to me." She swept out of the room, pointing her finger sternly at Alison who was about to protest. Through the closed door, the girls could hear her arguing with the reporter who was obviously not inclined to take no for an answer.

Alison crept quietly to the door and cautiously turned the knob.

"Close that door, if you know what's good for you," Jean ordered immediately. She had been standing facing the door, expecting just such a move from her daughter. As the door closed, they heard her say, "No, certainly not. And you still haven't told me where you got your information." She was almost a full ten minutes on the telephone before the girls heard her say loudly, "Definitely not. No. Under no circumstances, please leave us alone." She rang off.

Jean came back into the room, looking flushed and angry. "Damned cheek!"

Sarah looked at her with a worried expression, she had rarely seen her aunt so furious.

Alison looked fit to burst. "Why can't Sarah talk to the reporter,

Mum?" she asked aggressively. "I think you're being really mean; you're stopping her being really famous and being on television and stuff. It's not fair." She angrily threw herself into a chair.

"I don't really mind talking to her," Sarah volunteered timidly.

"No!" Jean snapped. "Don't be so silly both of you; you don't have any idea what you're talking about." She turned to Alison, "You prattle on about being famous; she's not going to make Sarah famous, she's going to make her ridiculous. She's going to sensationalise what happened and make Sarah seem like some sort of freak who has hallucinations or something."

Sarah sat silently, quite overwhelmed and feeling as if she were going to cry.

Alison flounced around in her chair, muttering, "I bet she would've got pots of money for being interviewed as well."

"What I want to know," Jean fumed, "is where she got the story from. I asked her several times but she just kept on saying, 'We do not reveal our sources'," Jean mimicked the reporter's strong Glasgow accent.

Calming down a little, she tried to explain. "Look," she said to Sarah, "I made you promise not to have anything more to do with the castle or the stupid mystery because you've had a very frightening and dangerous experience and I didn't want you to upset yourself any more. I just didn't think it was healthy for you to be wrapped up so much in talk of ghosts and spirits. I was really frightened you might have some sort of nervous breakdown or something; then what happens? First we have to go all through it for Sergeant Campbell and then, when you've hardly had a chance to forget about it, we have that dreadful woman on the phone, wanting to come and interview you. I'm not going to allow that under any circumstances. Apart from any other consideration, your father would go absolutely mad. He'd probably refuse to let you come again and we both love you and want you here with us."

She smiled and pulled a funny little face at Sarah who stood up and hugged her.

Alison looked contrite and her resentment faded. "Anyway," she said, "I bet she wouldn't really have paid us anything."

***

As the girls were preparing for bed, Jean worried in case the upsets of the evening had re-awakened in Sarah frightening memories of her ordeal. But the girls talked for about half an hour then fell asleep. A little while later, Jean came up herself and looked in on them. She was relieved to find Sarah in a deep untroubled sleep.

***

In the early hours of the morning, as Sarah slept soundly, she heard a faint voice, as if from far away, calling her name again and again.

Chapter 11

The following morning at breakfast, Jean announced that it was supermarket day. "If we clear up quickly and get off as soon as we can, we should be back by lunchtime."

"Oh, Mum! Can't we do what we did last time, go round the shops and to the cinema?" Alison whined.

"Look here, I can't afford to do that sort of thing every week. In any case, I want to get back. I've got a lot of work I must get on with, I've got rather behind this last week what with one thing and another."

"Well, surely we don't have to come, then? It's so boring just sitting in the car for hours."

Jean pursed her lips and raised her eyes to heaven. "How many times have I told you that I need somebody to help me with all the groceries? It's so unfair of you to expect me to do it all on my own when I've got two great galumphing girls hanging about here doing nothing; you're coming and that's that."

"Well, we wouldn't necessarily be doing nothing," Alison said cunningly, "we could stay here and tidy up the house. Then you could get straight off and be back even quicker."

"That still doesn't give me any help at the supermarket, does it? Since when have you been so keen on doing housework?"

"It's better than sitting in the boring car all that time," Alison answered sullenly.

"I've got an idea," Sarah volunteered. "Why don't I come with you to the supermarket and Alison can stay here and do the cleaning?"

"Hey! No way! That means I'll have to do it all on my own."

"Well, it's either that or the supermarket," Jean said firmly. "Take your pick. I don't mind which way as long as I have some help with the shopping."

"Oh, all right then, I'll stay here," Alison grumbled. "Although I think it's a bit much, expecting me to do the whole house on my own."

***

After breakfast, Sarah and Jean left in the car to drive to the supermarket in Fort William. Left on her own, Alison reluctantly set about the list of chores which her mother had left for her. She cleared away the breakfast things and washed up, after which she wiped down all the worktops and cupboards in the kitchen. She helped the work along by howling off-key to music on the kitchen radio and wriggling her body in a gawky dance as she worked but, without her mother's presence to supervise and keep her going, she soon began to tire of the routine jobs and decided that she needed a cup of coffee and a slice of toast and jam.

She was sitting at the kitchen table when the front doorbell rang. Wondering who the caller could be, she rose from the table and went into the hall. Through the patterned glass of the front door, she could see the figure of a youngish woman.

Alison opened the door and smiled at the smartly dressed stranger. "I'm afraid my mother's out at the moment."

The woman gave her a dazzling smile. "Oh, dear. Never mind, perhaps you can help me. Are you Sarah?"

"No, I'm Alison, Sarah's my cousin," she replied helpfully,

"Oh, I see. Is Sarah not at home either, then?" In fact, she had been sitting in her car in a field gateway just above the house for nearly an hour and had seen Jean and Sarah drive away. She had been hoping to get one of the girls on her own if they had left the house, but seeing Jean drive off with one of them suited her plans even better. She had waited a little longer, just to make sure that Jean was not coming back, before coming to the door.

"I'm afraid she's gone shopping with my mother," Alison answered apologetically. "They've gone to Fort William and they won't be back until lunchtime."

"Well, can I have a chat with you instead?" The woman smiled her winning smile again. "I'm Susan Riley from the Glasgow Sunday Post. Would you mind if I come in for a minute?" Without waiting for an answer, she stepped into the hall.

"Er, yes, certainly," Alison said in confusion, overwhelmed by the woman's breezy confidence. She hesitantly led the way to the sitting room. "Would you like to come in here and have a seat?"

The reporter entered the room and looked around. "What a lovely room," she said, seating herself in an armchair, "your mother must have wonderful taste."

Alison flushed with pleasure. She was going to say that her mother did not want her to have anything to do with reporters but after the compliment she felt it would be rude.

The woman relaxed in the armchair smiling at her.

Alison wondered what to say next. "Um, what did you want to talk to me about, Miss Riley?" she began hesitantly.

The reporter leaned forward and patted Alison's hand, smiling.

"Call me Sue. It makes me feel so old if you call me Miss Riley. After all we are not that far apart in age are we?" She giggled girlishly.

Alison looked at her in surprise and could not quite believe that.

"I'll tell you what though," Susan Riley continued. "I've driven such a long way this morning, and I could just murder a cup of coffee."

"Yes, of course," Alison said hastily, feeling embarrassed as if the suggestion was a criticism of her graciousness as a hostess, "I'll just be a moment."

Alison boiled the kettle for two mugs of coffee. Whatever was she going to do about this reporter woman? She knew her mother wouldn't have let her in the house in the first place but it seemed as though she was inside before Alison could think what to do.

She tried to think of ways to tell her to go away but the reporter was so pleasant and friendly that everything that she could think of to say seemed impossibly rude. In addition, Alison had never met a reporter before, and she was in fact rather in awe of her visitor. On television it always seemed such a glamorous job that she'd often day-dreamed about being a famous international correspondent herself. On the other hand, her mother was going to be absolutely furious with her. Perhaps she'll go away when she's had her coffee, she thought. She picked up the two mugs and carried them through to the sitting room.

To her horror she saw that Susan Riley was relaxing in the armchair smoking. Her mother hated the smell of tobacco smoke and would have a fit if all her furniture and curtains smelled of cigarettes.

"Er, excuse me," Alison said awkwardly, "but my mother hates cigarette smoke in the house."

Sue Riley raised her eyebrows and laughed in amusement. "Oh, I see. Well, we mustn't upset Mummy, must we?" She held the cigarette up in the air with a brittle smile and looked vaguely about her for an ashtray.

Her face flushed red with embarrassment; Alison looked around wildly for the ashtray she knew wasn't there. "I'm sorry," she stuttered, "I don't think there is an ashtray."

The reporter sat watching her with raised eyebrows and a half smile. "I've got an idea," she said sweetly, holding out the cigarette. "Why don't you give me the coffee cups and then you take this and throw it away somewhere?"

Alison scuttled off to the kitchen in relief and disposed of the cigarette in the bin.

Sitting in a chair opposite Sue Riley, Alison clutched her mug of coffee in both hands, she looked timidly at the woman who was sipping her coffee and smiling at her.

"Er, what was it that you wanted to talk to me about?" she asked, desperately.

"Well, I was hoping your mother would grant me an interview with Sarah."

Before Alison could answer she went on. "It's such an exciting story, I just know that our readers would be thrilled to read all about it and it would make Sarah quite a celebrity. You too," she added.

"I'm ever so sorry, but Mum doesn't want Sarah to talk about it in case it upsets her." Alison couldn't, from politeness, bring herself to mention her mother's opinion of reporters.

"Oh, that is a pity!" Sue replied with a disappointed expression, just as if it was news to her. "I was hoping she'd change her mind if I could talk to her in person."

Alison saw a chance to be rid of her visitor. "She'll be back at lunchtime if you could come back this afternoon," she said, hurriedly.

"Oh, dear, I'm afraid that would be too late," Sue sighed with regret. "You see I'd miss my deadline for Sunday's edition. You understand about deadlines?"

"Oh, er, yes. Yes, of course," Alison assured her, trying to sound as if newspaper jargon was totally familiar to her, "I'm sorry your journey's been wasted."

Sue smiled wistfully. "Oh, well, it can't be helped, can it?" She looked around her as if preparing to leave, but without actually standing up. "I'm so disappointed. You see it's such a wonderful story and I was really depending on it." She looked downcast. "You see I am only employed for a trial period at the paper, and this story would have been my big break. My editor wouldn't have been able to sack me if I'd been able to get this interview. It's very hard for a girl to succeed in a man's world like newspapers." She looked as if she was going to cry.

Alison felt a rush of sympathy for the poor woman. "I really am terribly sorry," she blurted out, "but Mum won't be back in time."

"There's nothing for it, then," Sue said in resignation, "I suppose I shall just have to go back and face the music." Her shoulders slumped in misery; then she looked up with an expression of hope, "Unless you would give me an interview?"

"Me? Well, I don't know," Alison stuttered.

"Oh, please say yes," Sue begged, "it would mean such a lot to my career."

Alison was completely confused by the need to choose between her mother's wrath and the chance to save this poor woman's job. "What do you want me to tell you?" she said uncertainly.

The reporter brightened visibly. "Oh that's so sweet of you, thank you so much. I knew you were a nice person as soon as I met you."

Alison blushed. Despite knowing, deep down, that she ought not to be doing it, Alison found herself telling the whole story to the reporter. From time to time the woman interrupted her to ask questions although, somewhat to Alison's surprise, she did not take notes. She told her about their first visit to the castle and Sarah's strange vision, how Sarah had walked in her sleep and had become convinced the soul of Hamish Grant was asking her for help; about Constable Jamieson's theory and how Sarah had been determined to return to the castle. Finally, she related the events of two days before, Sarah's ordeal and rescue and her account of her vision of the murder of Hamish Grant.

When Alison had finished her story, Susan Riley looked at her with a strangely elated smile. "I can't tell you how much I appreciate what you've told me. You have really done me a big favour." She stood up to leave.

"Er, what are you going to write about Sarah?" asked Alison anxiously, now quite sure that she had done something really stupid.

"Oh, don't worry about that," said the reporter airily, "it's probably just background material." She smiled winningly at Alison again. "You know."

Alison nodded dumbly.

"Anyway, I must dash now. Thanks again," and with a patronising pat on Alison's cheek, she made for the front door and down the drive to her car.

Alison watched her drive away, feeling sick with worry.

"Mum will murder me when she comes home," she wailed quietly to herself. She thought of running off somewhere and hiding like a naughty little child but she realised that it wouldn't help. "Perhaps they won't print anything and Mum will never find out," she muttered. "It's not as if we have that paper anyway." Slightly cheered by the thought that she might, after all, avoid being found out, she closed the door.

"Oh, God, the cigarette!" she shrieked. She ran to the kitchen and retrieved the cigarette from the waste bin and shredded it up in the sink, flushing the bits down the plughole. She found the kitchen air freshener and sprayed some into the bin and then ran into the sitting room and smothered the curtains, carpet and chairs with it. Noticing the time, she flung herself into the task of completing all the chores so as not to give her mother any reason to suspect she had spent the morning other than in honest toil.

When Jean and Sarah returned with the groceries, they were surprised to find Alison industriously ironing.

"You have been busy." Jean looked around in pleased approval.

"Oh yes," Alison replied casually, "and I just thought I'd help you by doing a bit of the ironing as well."

"Well, that's a nice surprise, thank you," her mother said.

Sarah wrinkled her nose. "Terrible pong of air freshener."

Jean looked at Alison with raised eyebrows.

"Oh, I er. I burnt a piece of toast," she explained quickly.

***

Susan Riley drove quickly back towards Glasgow with a jubilant smile on her face. Seeing a village telephone box, she pulled up next to it.

"Hallo, Auntie Flora? It's Susan," she said. "Bingo! I've got the lot. What? No, the Frazer girl, Alison." After a few more words, she rang off and resumed her journey.

In the hallway of her house in Kilmore, Mrs Forbes replaced the telephone with a satisfied smile.

Chapter 12

Sergeant Campbell sat at the breakfast table, reading his Sunday newspaper. After a glance at the front page, he turned to the sports pages at the back. He read the Saturday football reports before turning again to the front of the newspaper. After quickly scanning the front page he turned over and started to read.

He shot bolt upright in his chair. "Oh, damn!" he swore. "This has really put the cat among the pigeons." He read the article again and sat back in his chair thinking, with a grim expression on his face.

Standing up, he reached for his jacket, draped over the back of a chair, "I'm just popping out for a wee while, Maggie," he called, and pausing only to pick up his cap, he hurried out to his van.

***

Jean was surprised to see the sergeant standing on her doorstep. "Hallo, Mr Campbell, what brings you here so early on a Sunday morning?"

"Do you mind if I come in for a word, Mrs Frazer?"

Jean suddenly felt alarmed by his serious expression. "Yes, of course, come in. Has something happened?"

Sergeant Campbell nodded towards the sitting room. "Perhaps we could talk in private," he suggested.

Jean followed him into the sitting room and closed the door behind them. She stood silently watching the sergeant.

"Mrs Frazer," he began, "have you seen the newspaper this morning?"

Jean shook her head. "I've only had time to glance at the headlines so far; why, what's the matter?" Suddenly, she was sure that it was bad news about Stewart and her heart lurched.

"I don't know if you have *The Sunday Post*," he continued, "but maybe you'd better read this first." He handed her the newspaper folded at the right place.

Jean started to read and then made a small sound of dismay and sat down suddenly. What she read made her head spin:

TEENAGE GIRL SOLVES WAR-TIME MYSTERY! WAR-HERO MURDERED SHE CLAIMS!

A young girl was saved from a macabre death by suffocation due to the intuition and prompt action of castle guide Mrs Flora Forbes. The girl, Sarah Hale, had gone to Craig Dubh Castle, Argyllshire, in the hope of solving the mysterious war-time disappearance of Hamish Grant, a 27 year old Naval Lieutenant and the last laird of the castle.

The girl, who had already shown psychic powers, claims to have seen a vision of the missing man being murdered in his own room by a beautiful woman. In a bizarre twist, the girl was so frightened by what she had seen, she concealed herself in an antique oak chest and became locked in. As the castle was closed for the night, she would surely have suffocated but fortunately, for her, on hearing of the girl's disappearance, from her distraught aunt, Jean Frazer, 34, Mrs Forbes immediately recalled the girl.

"I remember thinking she looked very strange, as if she was not all there," said Mrs Forbes to this reporter.

"When her aunt came to me in a panic, I decided to search the castle, assisted by the local police officer. Knowing the girl was obsessed by the mystery, I overruled his plan to search the castle from the cellars to the roof and insisted we should go straight to the tower room. While the officer searched elsewhere, I had an inspired theory that I would find her in the antique iron bound chest and so it proved. If we had delayed to search the rest of the castle first," she added, "the poor girl would have certainly died of suffocation."

This newspaper understands that Mrs Forbes is to be considered for an award for her prompt and vital action.

"That would be very nice but is quite unnecessary for just doing my duty," Mrs Forbes commented modestly. "I would have been quite happy with a simple thank you from the girl or her relatives but sadly I haven't heard a word from them."

***

Jean continued to read while the sergeant watched patiently. When she had finished, she crumpled the paper into her lap with both of her hands and stared at him.

"I don't understand; where did this come from?"

"I was going to ask you that," he said.

"But I spoke to the reporter on the phone and refused point blank to allow her to interview Sarah; I don't understand where she's got all this from."

"Well, I can tell you how she got hold of the story; you see, Susan Riley is Mrs Forbes' niece. I recognised the name immediately."

"Yes, but Mrs Forbes didn't know anything about what Sarah thinks she saw in the castle and all the other details," Jean said, puzzled. "Only…"

"Yes, exactly. Only the four of us here knew," the sergeant finished for her grimly.

"But, the girls knew I wouldn't permit any interviews; we talked about it on Thursday evening when that dreadful woman telephoned. I explained carefully, to them both, why I didn't want anything in the papers."

"Well, one of them talked, I am afraid."

"But, that's impossible; they haven't been out of my sight." She paused horrified, "Except…" She shot upright and crossed quickly to the door. "Alison!" she shrieked. "Get in here immediately!"

Alison's blonde head appeared round the door and she slowly edged into the room. Her face was very white and her eyes seemed unnaturally large and round as she looked apprehensively from the grim-faced sergeant to her furious mother.

Jean held the folded newspaper, arms outstretched. "Do you know anything about this?"

Alison tried to swallow but her throat had gone very dry, "No, Mum," she croaked.

"You're lying to me, aren't you?" her mother yelled furiously. "You were the only one left alone while Sarah and I did the shopping. I thought you looked shifty when I got back. I should've known you'd been up to something. Why did you do it? Why did you talk to that awful woman when I specifically told you not to?"

Alison began to cry. "She tricked me into letting her in and she wouldn't go away," she howled.

"Yes, but why did you have to tell her anything?" Jean shouted in frustration. "I would like to shake you until your teeth rattle you stupid, stupid girl."

"I couldn't help it, Mum, honestly. She said she'd get the sack if she didn't get an interview and I felt sorry for her," Alison sobbed.

The sergeant cleared his throat and, looking at Jean, he jerked his head almost imperceptibly from Alison to the door.

Jean swallowed her anger and pulled herself together. "Go straight to your room. Now! I'll come up and deal with you later."

After the door had closed behind her pathetic bent shoulders the sergeant said, "Don't be too hard on the lassie, Mrs Frazer, she's only young and newspaper reporters are absolutely ruthless. She would've told her anything to trick her into talking. The lassie didn't really stand a chance, as many a lot older and wiser than her have found out to their cost."

"Oh, I suppose so," Jean said miserably. "But it's just what I wanted to prevent; Sarah will never live this down. God! I could kill that Forbes woman and her foul niece. I wish I could sue them for libel or something."

"I don't think you'd have much of a case, I'm afraid, and of course it would attract even more attention. At least the story will probably be forgotten in a week and it won't be seen in England unless one of the big daily papers gets interested. Let's just keep our fingers crossed they don't."

"Yes, you're right of course," Jean agreed reluctantly. "It's no use crying over spilt milk. I expect it will all blow over."

Sergeant Campbell regarded her thoughtfully. "Yes, but to tell you the truth, it isn't that which worries me. It's the bit at the end. After they rehash the story of Hamish Grant disappearing."

Jean picked up the paper and scanned through the article again.

"That bit," he said pointing.

This reporter understands that the police had a suspect at the time of Mr Grant's disappearance but could never prove their case. It is now believed that the inquiry is to be re-opened in the light of the new evidence supplied by Sarah Hale. An arrest may be imminent.

The report went on to mention other cases of crimes supposedly solved as a result of evidence supplied by clairvoyants and psychics.

Jean looked at Sergeant Campbell. "But that's rubbish, isn't it? I thought no one had any idea what happened to him."

"Yes, you're quite right, they didn't; but aren't you forgetting what Willie Jamieson told the girls?"

"About how he suspected murder? Well, yes, but isn't this just newspaper sensationalism? I don't see why you are worried by it."

The sergeant took her arm and sat her in the chair again. "Look, Mrs Frazer, I don't want to frighten you but you haven't thought it through."

"Thought what through?" Jean interrupted.

"Well, let's just assume for a minute that Hamish Grant was murdered," he said carefully. "Then the chances are that the murderer is still alive, after all, most of the other people involved are."

Jean nodded.

"Don't you see? If the murderer sees that article, then he or she might believe it's true."

"Oh, but surely not?" Jean said in disbelief. "Any sensible person would see through that article immediately. They surely wouldn't believe it for a minute?"

Sergeant Campbell looked grave. "Isn't that the point, Mrs Frazer? We are talking about a murderer not a nice sensible person. Someone who has killed once already and may now believe that he or she is about to be caught after getting away with it all these years."

Jean looked at him in alarm. "What are you saying?"

"I'm saying that if all this is true and there is a murderer loose out there, then he or she may decide to try and get rid of the only supposed witness."

Jean stared at him in horror. "You can't mean Sarah?" she said faintly. "She isn't a witness; she just thought that she'd seen a vision of a murder. It wouldn't be evidence, you said so yourself."

"Agreed," he replied grimly, "but, remember, we're talking about someone who is possibly deranged. Rules of evidence wouldn't mean much to someone like that."

Jean slumped in the chair and covered her face with her hands. "Oh, my God, what are we going to do?"

Sergeant Campbell looked down at the distressed woman and tried to reassure her. "The first thing we have to do is to keep things in perspective," he told her encouragingly. "For a start, we're only assuming that a murder took place at all. There's absolutely no evidence to even suppose that such a thing ever happened. We've built up the whole thing from nothing more than a young rookie constable's suspicions at the time and the imagination of an impressionable young girl."

"But why did you suggest that Sarah is in danger, if you don't believe it?" Jean asked, in confusion.

"Because I just want you to be on your guard. I didn't want to say any of this to frighten you but I had to make sure you understood so that you watch the lassie as much as you can."

"But, can't the police do anything to protect her?"

Sergeant Campbell made a wry face. "What can I tell them at Fort William, Mrs Frazer? They're not going to supply men as bodyguards because a young girl says she had a vision. All I can say is that I'll do all I can to be around as much as possible. I want you to watch her like a hawk and phone if you see the slightest thing suspicious. It doesn't matter if it turns out to be a false alarm; in fact I'll be only too pleased if it does. I'll leave word with Maggie so she knows exactly where I am at all times and I'll phone you regularly, just to confirm everything is all right. I expect you'll get sick of the sight of me and my van in the next few weeks," he smiled.

Jean made an effort to smile back. "Thank you, Mr Campbell, I know you'll do your best. I just wish that Stewart was here."

***

Up at Kilmore House, Morag McDonald finished washing the breakfast dishes. Straightening her stiff back with a sigh, she decided to have a rest for half an hour and read the Sunday paper. Moving slowly, because of her troublesome arthritis, she walked over to the kitchen fire and sat down with relief in her old armchair. She glanced briefly at the headlines and then turned over the page. What she saw made her gasp in astonishment. Painfully, she got up from the chair and slowly made her way upstairs to her mistress's bedroom.

Mrs Grant was sitting at the dressing table, brushing her hair. She looked up in surprise as the elderly maid entered without knocking.

"Madam! Madam!" Morag cried. "Just look at this in the paper," and she gave an open copy of the *Glasgow Sunday Post* to the wife of Hamish Grant!

Chapter 13

Sergeant Campbell's warning left Jean in a terrible predicament. If she told Sarah she might be in danger from Hamish Grant's supposed murderer, it would surely terrify her. On the other hand, as the sergeant had pointed out, there was no evidence at all that Hamish Grant had been murdered or was even actually dead. The whole idea had been based on nothing more than an old policeman's hunch and Sarah's vision. Could she, on this flimsy evidence, terrify the girl with the prospect of being stalked by a murderer? How then could she explain why she didn't want the girls to roam about the countryside as they usually did, nor why she wanted them to keep close by at all times? She considered sending Sarah home, but to do so, without any apparent reason, would cause her great distress, and risk damaging irrevocably their loving relationship.

Jean went upstairs to see Alison. Her anger had abated considerably now she had had time to think about the policeman's plea. She realised it was too much to expect her to be able to deal with a pushy and unscrupulous professional journalist at her age. On the other hand, Alison was all too often headstrong and disobedient. It was, after all, entirely her fault that Sarah may be in danger and Jean was in such a difficult position.

As she entered Alison's room and saw the poor, tear-stained, young face looking up at her with wide, fearful eyes, she suddenly found herself feeling very sorry for her. At the same time, Jean could not help thinking what a wonderful little actress her daughter was. No heart could fail to be melted by the pathetic woebegone expression she wore, but Jean forced herself to look stern and angry.

"I cannot tell you what harm you may have caused Sarah by your stupidity," she began, with more truth than she could admit to.

"I'm really, really sorry, Mum," Alison said pitifully. "I really didn't mean to but she sort of tricked me into telling her everything."

"It's just no good being sorry. Sorry, doesn't put things right again. If you'd just do as you are told for once and use some common sense, then none of this would have happened."

"It won't really harm Sarah, will it, Mum? I don't see how."

"Well, for a start, if the daily newspapers get hold of the story, Sarah will be made a nationwide laughing stock. Just think what would happen to her at school; she would be teased and bullied mercilessly by the other pupils and the teachers would probably class her as an unstable neurotic."

Alison looked mortified. "Honestly, I didn't mean to cause all this trouble."

"Well, to help you learn to act with more thought and common sense in future, you're going to spend the rest of the day in your room. And," Jean emphasised, "on your own too. You're not going to have Sarah up here with you to gossip and mess around."

Alison pretended to sulk, but, secretly, she was pleased to have got off so lightly.

Jean had a flash of inspiration. "Look! If this gets into the daily papers, we could find ourselves up to our ears in reporters in the next few days. Not only that, but heaven knows what sort of weirdos and cranks will be attracted as well."

Alison looked suitably impressed.

"I think for the time being, both of you should stay close to the house just in case. And I want you to keep a careful eye on Sarah all the time. If you see any strangers hanging around, come and tell me immediately."

Alison nodded enthusiastically, grateful for a chance to gain favour again. Besides, the prospect of defending Sarah from marauding reporters and lurking nut-cases began to seem rather exciting.

Pleased with her solution to the problem of keeping Sarah under close surveillance without frightening her, Jean went downstairs to the kitchen where Sarah had been keeping well out of the way. She repeated the warning that she had just given Alison and made her promise to keep close by the house.

"You see, darling, there are a lot of very odd people about who would be attracted by a story of murders and ghosts. Sensation seekers, like the ghouls who travel miles to gawp at aeroplane and train crashes, as well as cranks and the out-and-out nut-cases. I don't want you to be bothered by them, or pestered by reporters come to that."

Sarah nodded solemnly, her eyes wide as she dwelt on the thought of being pursued by a mob of loonies and journalists.

"What I want you to do for the next few days is to stay close to home and keep an eye out for any strangers hanging about. If you see anyone at all you don't recognise, come and tell me straight away."

***

For the next few days, the girls stayed dutifully in the house and garden, only venturing out with Jean for occasional walks on the hill or in the car. Jean was greatly reassured by the frequency with which she saw Sergeant Campbell's van, either cruising slowly up or down the lane by the house or around the village, when she took the girls to the shop with her.

Gradually, as the week wore on, it became obvious the press had not thought the story worth pursuing. There were no telephone calls or people calling at the house and the only strangers to be seen were late season tourists passing through the village. Jean felt her anxiety gradually ebb away and she became increasingly sure their fears had been groundless.

"I think it was really a false alarm," she told Sergeant Campbell when he telephoned.

"Aye, well, you may be right," he agreed. "Let's hope so anyway. Still, better safe than sorry."

On Thursday afternoon, Jean was making cakes when she realised she had run out of jam. The girls had been moping about the house all day, very bored and rather fed up that the expected hoards of lunatics hadn't materialised.

"I'm in a bit of a fix with this sponge," Jean said. "We'll have to drive down to the shop for some more jam but I'm stuck until this cake is done. I've only just put it in and I daren't leave it; it would be burned to a cinder by the time we got back. The trouble is the shop will be closed before the cake is ready."

Alison, who had been sitting at the table with her head on her forearms, sat up. "We'll go on our bikes," she said quickly. "I'm absolutely bored stiff sitting around here."

Jean shook her head immediately, "No! You know what we agreed."

"Yes, but, Mum," Alison whined, "there aren't any weirdos hanging about, or reporters. We haven't seen anybody all week."

Jean hesitated. It was quite true there had been no cause for alarm and the girls couldn't remain cooped up forever.

"Well, all right," she said uncertainly, "but I want you to go straight to the shop and then come straight home again. No hanging about in the village or wandering off anywhere else."

"Oh, great." The two girls shot up from the table.

"Wait while I get my money," said Sarah, "I want to buy a bar of chocolate."

They got their bicycles out of the shed and set off down the lane in high spirits, glad to be free again. Half-way to the village, there was a loud hiss from Sarah's front tyre. She wobbled violently and came to a halt.

"Stop! My tyre's burst," she called to Alison, who was riding ahead.

Alison looked round, then turned and rode back. "How did that happen?" She marvelled at the two inch slit in the side of the tyre.

"I'm not sure," Sarah turned to look back. "There must have been a broken bottle or a piece of metal or something."

"We'd better go back," Alison said, getting off her bicycle and preparing to walk.

Sarah was suddenly faced by the bleak prospect of no chocolate. "No, you go on and get the jam and I'll start walking back."

"Better not." Alison remembered her promise to her mother. "I'll come with you or Mum will go mad."

"Don't be stupid," Sarah urged. "If I start walking now, you'll catch me up miles before I get back home, then you can walk with me the rest of the way. If I give you the money, you can get me a bar of chocolate."

Alison looked doubtful. "Oh, well, if you think you'll be all right?"

"Of course I'm all right. Just stop messing around and go and get the stuff while I start walking. And don't forget my chocolate."

Alison set off again, feeling certain she should have stayed with Sarah. She looked back once or twice but all she could see was Sarah wheeling her bicycle slowly along the deserted road. She pedalled on and quite soon reached the outskirts of the straggling village.

Sarah pushed her disabled bicycle along the edge of the road, glad to be outside the confines of her aunt's house and car. She felt a little guilty about disobeying Jean's instructions but consoled herself that Alison would catch her up soon. In any case, she thought, it's a lot of fuss about nothing. They hadn't seen any strangers hanging around or anyone even vaguely loony looking.

She found herself thinking about Hamish Grant again. Several times since her ordeal in the castle she had remembered the voice that she thought was calling her. Sometimes, when she was just falling asleep, she was not at all sure she didn't really hear it.

Lost in thought, she didn't notice a smart looking car approaching from behind. Hearing the crunch of gravel under its tyres, she looked up and pulled her bicycle onto the grass at the edge of the road. The car stopped next to her and the window purred quietly down. A handsome looking, middle-aged woman leaned across the passenger seat.

"Someone wants to know the way," Sarah said to herself.

"Hallo, you're Sarah Hale, aren't you?" The woman smiled pleasantly.

Sarah was suddenly on her guard and nodded warily. The woman didn't look loony so she was probably another reporter.

"You don't know me, but I've been thinking about coming to see you. What a coincidence meeting you like this."

"My tyre's burst," said Sarah by way of explanation for her presence.

"Well, hop in and I'll give you a lift home," the woman invited cheerfully. "We can put your bike in the boot."

"Thanks," Sarah said, stepping back a pace, "but I think I'd better walk."

"Oh, are you sure?" the woman said in a disappointed voice. "I was looking forward to having a chat with you. You see I read about you in *The Sunday Post*."

"My aunt said I mustn't talk to anybody about that," Sarah answered quickly.

"I don't think she'd have included me," the woman laughed. "I should have introduced myself. I'm Moira Grant."

Sarah was dumbfounded. Face to face with the dreaded Mrs Grant, except she looked rather nice and seemed it too.

"According to the paper, you had a nasty experience last week," Mrs Grant smiled sympathetically. "That dreadful Forbes woman really should stop filling people up with that silly story. It's not as if it was true, after all, and I'm quite sure it doesn't really bring in any more tourists."

"You mean the story about Hamish, I mean Mr Grant?" asked Sarah in astonishment.

Mrs Grant laughed. "Yes, the mystery disappearance and all that. It's all rubbish I'm afraid, my dear. It's just to bring in the tourists."

"I don't understand," Sarah said in amazement. "Everyone round here believes it."

Mrs Grant smiled ruefully. "Yes, well, I suppose they were meant to, at least to start with; during the war I mean."

Sarah looked baffled. "I still don't follow."

Mrs Grant arched her back. "Look here, won't you sit in the car? It's killing my neck, bending over like this."

After a moment's hesitation, Sarah lowered her bicycle to the grass and slipped into the passenger seat, leaving the door open.

"That's better." Mrs Grant rubbed the back of her neck.

"I can see you properly without being a contortionist."

"What did you mean about people being meant to think that there was a mystery?" Sarah urged.

Mrs Grant looked at her as if she was deciding something. "Well, let's say it was preferable to a public scandal. You have to remember that in those days especially, people thought they had a certain position to keep up. Public respect was important."

"A scandal?" Sarah was fascinated. "What sort of scandal?"

Mrs Grant laughed at her eager expression. "Well, I'm not sure I want it made public knowledge even after all this time."

Sarah's expression was one of almost comical curiosity.

Mrs Grant laughed again and patted her hand sympathetically. "I'll tell you what we'll do. Chuck your bike in the back and come up to Kilmore House for a cup of coffee. As you've had such a fright because of this silly story, I'll tell you a bit about it anyway."

"Oh, I can't," Sarah said glumly, "I told my aunt that I would come straight home. She would be worried if I didn't go straight back."

"Oh, what a shame. Still, if she's expecting you, you must get on back. But never mind, I'll come and see you one day and we'll have our chat."

"That'll be great," Sarah said with pleasure.

"Well, I'm off on holiday tonight for a month, but when I come back, I'll come and see you and let you into the real secret of Craig Dubh Castle."

"Oh, but that won't be any good," Sarah said in alarm, "I shan't be here then, I only live here during the holidays."

"Oh, I see. Well, perhaps we can make it some other time. The Christmas holidays perhaps? Anyway, you'd better be getting along or your aunt will start to worry where you have got to."

This is terrible, Sarah thought in a panic, I can't last out until Christmas without knowing the truth. "Couldn't you come home now?" she pleaded. "My aunt wouldn't mind and I shall go potty if I have to wait until Christmas."

Mrs Grant laughed, then looked at her watch. "I can't really, I'm late now. I'm just on my way back from taking my old housekeeper, Morag, to her sister's for the month and I've got such a lot to do before I go away."

"Ohh!" wailed Sarah. "This is terrible, I shall go mad if I don't find out what really happened."

Mrs Grant thought for a moment. "You know, what we could do if you like, is go up to Kilmore House for that coffee and you can phone your aunt; tell her where you are and ask her to come and fetch you and the bike in, say, an hour?"

Sarah hesitated for a moment but her desire to find out the truth of the mystery overwhelmed her. "Oh, yes, please. I'm sure it'll be all right."

"Oh good. That's settled. Well, open the boot and chuck your bike in and let's do that," Mrs Grant said cheerfully.

***

At that moment, Alison was only just emerging from the shop. She was furious, having been forced to wait for nearly ten minutes while old Mrs Laing complained at length to the postmistress. She was just getting on her bike when Sergeant Campbell's van drew up next to her.

He wound down his window and smiled. "Hallo, Alison, what brings you here?"

"I've just been to the shop for Mum. It's taken absolutely ages to get served."

The sergeant watched Mrs Laing sorting out her shopping bag on the pavement and muttering darkly to herself.

"I'm not surprised," he grinned. "And where's that cousin of yours today?"

Alison waved her hand vaguely. "She's back at home now and I better get going because Mum wanted this jam."

"Right you are, you get off home then," he said, putting the van into gear. "Tell your mum that she knows where to find me if she needs me."

"I will, 'bye," called Alison as she mounted her bicycle.

On the ride back, Alison started to worry about what her mother would say. Sarah was surely home by now or at least she would be by the time Alison arrived. Would her mother be very angry about her leaving Sarah alone?

"It's Sarah's fault anyway," she told herself, "she made me come just to get her rotten chocolate. I wanted to go back with her, I hope she's going to own up if there's a row." She pedalled harder, in the faint hope of at least arriving at the same time as her cousin. When she pushed her bike into the shed, she noticed Sarah's wasn't there. "I wonder what she's done with her bike?" she said to herself.

Alison entered the kitchen with the jam. Her mother was turning out a cake on to the rack to cool.

"You've been a long time, I was getting worried."

"Oh, I had to wait for hours to get served; the shop was full and that horrid old bat Mrs Laing was having a row about her pension book. Where's Sarah?"

Jean looked up sharply. "What do you mean, isn't she with you?"

Alison felt a cold rush of alarm. "Er, no. She had a burst tyre on the way and she had to come back. I thought she was here with you."

Jean's face went a ghastly white and the cake slipped from her hands and the plate broke with a crash on the rack.

"Oh, my God!" she shrieked. "What have you done?"

Alison went rigid with fear at her mother's reaction. "She made me, Mum; she said she'd be all right. Honestly!" she gabbled.

Jean stared, aghast, at her trembling daughter and then, pulling herself together with a great effort, she started for the door.

"Get out of my way. Quickly, quickly! I must get hold of Sergeant Campbell."

With trembling hands, she grabbed for the telephone and sent it tumbling to the floor with a crash. Crying with fear and frustration she crouched down and retrieved it, relieved to hear the familiar dialling tone. Her hands were shaking so much she could hardly dial the number.

"Hallo Mrs Campbell, it's Jean Frazer. Can I speak to your husband please? It's very urgent."

"I'm sorry, Mrs Frazer, but he's just now had a call to go out to one of the farms. They've had some sheep killed by a dog but he's left me the number, if you tell me what's the matter."

"It's Sarah; she's missing. Oh, please hurry."

"You ring off and I'll telephone the farm. They'll give him the message. Try not to worry dear, he'll sort it out."

***

It was nearly twenty minutes before Sergeant Campbell arrived at the remote hill farm. The farmer's wife was waiting at the gate with the message.

"Damn!" he swore. "Quickly! Where's your phone?" He ran across the yard, towards the house, followed by the farmer's wife.

Standing next to the telephone, trying to comfort her hysterical daughter, Jean snatched up the receiver on the first ring.

"Oh, Sergeant Campbell, thank God! Sarah's disappeared." She quickly told him what had happened.

"Listen carefully, Mrs Frazer, I want you to ring my wife immediately and tell her to phone the number I left with her and give them the message. Have you got that?"

"Yes, but what are we going to do?" shrieked Jean.

"I've made some preparations in case this happened, Mrs Frazer. You just make the call; my wife knows what I want her to do. And, Mrs Frazer, I want you to stay by the phone."

"No! I can't, I'm going to look for Sarah," she said wildly, "I'm not stopping here doing nothing."

"Do as I say," he barked at her. "You're wasting time. I want you where I can contact you and you must look after your daughter. Now, make that call." He rang off.

Without a further word, he ran out of the open door and across the yard to his van. He revved the engine unmercifully and, with a squeal of protesting tyres, turned the vehicle round and shot off down the narrow road.

Chapter 14

Mrs Grant stopped her car on the gravel forecourt in front of the imposing front door. Sarah got out and looked up at the gloomy looking stone mansion.

Mrs Grant inserted her key into the lock. "Come in and phone your aunt." They entered a rather dark, mahogany panelled hall with heavy antique furniture around the walls.

"Do you think it would be better if I talked to your aunt in case she's upset about you not going straight home?"

Sarah, who, after her initial rush of optimism, had not been looking forward to making the call, smiled gratefully and nodded.

"Well, you go into the sitting room and make yourself comfortable and I'll ring her now."

Sarah went into the sitting room and sank down into an enormous armchair. She heard Mrs Grant dialling and then heard her speaking to her aunt.

"Hallo, Mrs Frazer? This is Moira Grant. I'm at Kilmore House and I've got Sarah with me. She had a burst tyre and I've brought her bike back here in the car. I'm just ringing you in case you were worried about her… Oh yes, well that's quite understandable. I hope you don't mind but I've offered her a cup of coffee and we're going to have a chat about the castle and the mystery. She's absolutely fascinated by it, isn't she?"

Mrs Grant listened. "Oh, it's no trouble, but the thing is I'm going away tonight and I'm in rather a rush. Could you come and pick her up to save me coming out again?… You can? Oh fine. I'll look forward to meeting you."

She came into the sitting room smiling. "That's all right, then. She didn't seem to mind. She's going to come and fetch you in about an hour. You stay here and I'll go and make the coffee."

Left alone, Sarah gazed round the room. It was obviously furnished very expensively and was really rather cosy, although it didn't look quite 'lived in', she thought. There was a huge oil painting of hairy, Highland cattle, with giant curving horns, above the carved mahogany mantelpiece. There was a big comfy sofa and armchairs and lots of little antique tables with lace cloths, covered by dozens of pretty china figures and pots.

On a side table there was a group of photographs in silver frames. The largest was a picture of a beautiful young woman with an old fashioned hairstyle. Sarah had the strange feeling she had seen it before somewhere.

Mrs Grant came into the room carrying a silver tray upon which were two mugs of coffee, a plate of biscuits and a jug of cream.

"I didn't know how you like your coffee," she said, "I like mine rather strong so I brought some extra cream in case it's too bitter for you."

Sarah accepted the proffered mug with both hands. "It does look a bit black, Can I have a lot of cream?"

"Shall I take it back to the kitchen and put some more water in it?" Mrs Grant held out her hand for the mug.

"Oh, no, don't bother, it'll be fine with lots of cream."

Mrs Grant sat in the other chair and they both drank their coffee and nibbled biscuits. Sarah thought her coffee was fairly awful but it was just about drinkable.

While they drank, Mrs Grant asked her about school and where she lived. "And where is your father?"

"He's in New York on business at the moment," Sarah told her. "He's just set up a new office there and he has to stay until everything is sorted out."

"What sort of business is he in?"

"He exports medical equipment all over the world," Sarah

answered politely, almost bursting with impatience to talk about the mystery.

"And you stay with your aunt while he's away, then?"

"No, only in the holidays; we have a housekeeper at home, called Mrs Jones." Sarah answered. She kept looking at the portrait of the young woman and wished she could remember where she had seen it before. She brushed her forehead with her hand. It's very hot in this room, she thought vaguely.

"I hope you don't mind me asking," she said, "but who is that in the portrait?"

Mrs Grant smiled at her. "That's a portrait of me when I was first married."

Suddenly, Sarah knew with awful certainty where she had seen that face before. It was the woman in her vision. The woman who had murdered Hamish Grant. She started to get up from the armchair but her legs felt wobbly and she sat down again with a jolt.

Mrs Grant was smiling at her but her eyes had a strange wide stare.

"So! It's all true, isn't it? You did see something at the castle, and now you've recognised me, haven't you?"

In panic, Sarah tried to get up but her legs felt numb and would not do as she wanted. "I have got to go now." Her voice was slurred and she had difficulty saying the words, as if she was drunk.

"Oh, no. I've got other plans for you." Mrs Grant smiled a twisted smile.

"My aunt will be here soon." Sarah struggled desperately to form the words.

Mrs Grant chuckled oddly. "I'm afraid not, my dear, you see nobody knows where you are. You are going to disappear without trace, just like dear Hamish. You wanted to find out what happened to him and I did promise to tell you, didn't I? Well, I am going to do better than that, I am going to show you."

Sarah whimpered and made another effort to stand up but this time she could not even raise herself from the chair.

"No, please don't," she said, but the words were hardly distinguishable.

Mrs Grant rose from her chair and walked over to where Sarah lay slumped in the armchair. "Now we have to hurry," she said to the barely conscious girl. "I really do have a plane to catch and as I said, I have a lot to do first."

Bending forward, she put her hands under Sarah's armpits and lifted the helpless girl to her feet. With her arm round Sarah's shoulders she half dragged, half walked her out into the hall then outside to the waiting car. She opened the rear door and pushed Sarah across the back seat, then covered her with a rug. She got in, started the engine and drove quickly away down the curving drive. At the bottom, she turned left, towards the coast. After about half a mile, she stopped the car and ran round to the boot. Grasping the bicycle, she threw it over the hedge into a tangled plantation of young conifers. They drove on very fast.

Sarah was only dimly aware of movement as she drifted in and out of consciousness. She felt the car stop again and thought she heard the scrape of a wooden gate being opened.

Mrs Grant drove the car into the castle courtyard and then closed the great wooden gate behind them. She hurried up the stone steps and opened the main door with her key. Leaving it ajar, she returned to the car and began the difficult task of pulling the helpless girl out of the back seat. Holding her as before, she slowly propelled Sarah towards the steps and then up to the door. She was flushed and gasping with the effort of virtually carrying the semi-conscious girl but, somehow, she was able to summon huge reserves of energy as she dragged Sarah up the last step and into the hall.

Mrs Grant draped Sarah's arm across her shoulders and held her wrist with one hand. Putting her other arm across Sarah's back, she supported the girl under the arm and they slowly inched their way across the hall and down the passage to the armoury. When they reached the foot of the spiral staircase, she realised that it was not wide enough for them both to climb.

She lowered Sarah to the floor and turned her round, so that her back was to the staircase. She sat on the second step and, grasping the girl beneath the arms, began to pull her up the stairs backwards, a step at a time.

***

Sergeant Campbell drove like a man possessed, hurling the van round the twists and turns of the narrow roads. The equipment in the back of the van broke loose from its straps and slid dangerously around as he flung the vehicle through the bends.

He thought about the missing girl and his foreboding of danger. "Willie was right all along. Why didn't anyone listen to him at the time? Then this poor little lassie wouldn't be in mortal danger now."

The van skidded dangerously as he hauled it round a steep uphill hairpin bend.

He reached the iron gate at the entrance to Kilmore House. Barely slowing down, he hurled the van between the two stone pillars and roared up the gravel drive, skidding to a halt outside the front door. He ran up the steps and banged on the door. The house was in darkness in the gathering twilight and he could neither see nor hear any movement. He ran round to the back of the house but all was securely locked. He continued around to the front again, peering into the ground floor windows.

When he came to the sitting room, he took out his truncheon and with two quick blows smashed the glass. Reaching through, he unlocked the sash window and climbed in. He crossed quickly over to the tray on the table and put his hand on one of the mugs; it was still warm. Sergeant Campbell ran into the hall and started to throw open the doors leading into the other rooms, then stopped.

"I'm in the wrong place," he said aloud. "It's got to be the castle."

He ran out of the front door and jumped into the van. Revving the engine hard he swung the vehicle round and, with his wheels spinning on the gravel, he raced down the drive to the road and turned towards the coast.

***

Mrs Grant had reached the middle of the second flight of steps but her breath was now coming in painful wheezing gasps and she felt as though her head was exploding with each beat of her heart. She stopped hauling the body of the helpless girl for a moment and rested her head against the cold stone. Her pulse beat in her ears like a great drum.

"Hurry, I must hurry, no time to rest," she gasped and, summoning up new reserves of strength, she began to inch her way backwards up the spiral staircase.

Suddenly, there was no stone at her back any more; she had reached the top. Sobbing with exhaustion, she knelt on the floor of the passage and dragged Sarah up the last few steps. Pressing her hands on the rough stonework she pulled herself to her feet. Swaying unsteadily, she bent and tried to lift Sarah up but she was too far gone to manage it. She put her hands beneath Sarah's arms and began to drag her along the passage.

***

Sergeant Campbell drove very fast across the causeway. Leaping from the van, he tried the little door set into the main gate and his heart sank when it would not move. He tried the black iron knob on the big gate and felt a rush of relief as it swung open easily. Mrs Grant's car was parked in the yard. A crack of light spilled from the castle door. He ran across the courtyard and up the steps, crashing open the heavy door. The hall was deserted but the light was on in the armoury passage. He ran down the passage and into the armoury. The lights were on but the room was deserted.

"She's up in the tower," he said to himself and began to run towards the spiral staircase at the far end.

***

Her task done, Mrs Grant leaned against the rough stone wall, her head pounding. The beating of her heart seemed to shake her body with its violence and every breath seemed to burn in her chest.

"Hurry, must get away," she gasped, and began to stagger towards the stairs. At the top, she reached for the handrope and nearly fell. Grasping it with both hands, she began to inch her way down, keeping close to the wall where the steps were widest. She had nearly reached the bottom of the upper flight of steps when she heard a door bang somewhere below, followed by the sound of running footsteps. Moaning to herself in panic and exhaustion, Mrs Grant turned around and began to ascend the stairs as fast as she could. Reaching the top again, she staggered along the passage looking for somewhere to hide.

"The tower room," she mumbled, thinking of the oak door with its iron lock. She leaned against the stone doorway and fumbled with the huge iron key. Turning it with both hands, she pushed the door open and almost fell into the room beyond.

The room was in darkness as, sobbing with relief, she threw herself against the heavy door and slid the huge iron bolt home. Gasping painfully for breath, she straightened up and reached for the light switch.

Suddenly, she was aware that the room was filled with a warm red glow from a peat fire in the massive stone fireplace. Looking up, her eyes widened with fear and she screamed as Hamish Grant said,

"Hallo, Moira, I've waited a long time for you."

Chapter 15

Sergeant Campbell leapt up the smooth, sloping steps, two at a time, grabbing at the handrope with every stride. Reaching the first floor, he paused for a second to listen. Above the sound of his own gasping breath, he thought he heard footsteps on the flagstones above, then the sound of a heavy door slamming. He raced up the second flight of stairs and into the passage next to the garderobe. Hardly pausing to glance inside, he ran quickly to the door of the tower room and tried the handle; it did not move. He grabbed at the huge key and twisted it but it was obviously unlocked already. Turning the handle again he threw his weight at the massive oak door. It didn't budge. He stood back. "That's no good. She's bolted it on the inside."

"Open the door, please, Mrs Grant," he called, hammering on the thick oak planks. "It's no use, come out and give me the young lassie." There was no sound from inside the locked room so he hammered again and shouted, "It's all over, Mrs Grant. Don't be foolish, come out now with the girl."

Sergeant Campbell stood in front of the door, his chest heaving. "I'll have to force the door," he gasped. "I'll find something in the van."

He ran back to the top of the staircase and leapt down the steps, several at a time, grabbing at the handrope to save himself from falling. Reaching the armoury he ran along the passage to the hall and then out of the door and across the courtyard.

He flung open the back of the van and began to throw out the tangle of disordered equipment, looking for an axe and a long crowbar. He found the axe and just as he was pulling the crowbar clear, headlights swung onto the causeway and a police Land Rover squealed to a halt behind the van. Two young constables jumped out and ran up to him.

"We got here as soon as we could, Sarge," one of them said. "Sergeant McKay's gone up to Kilmore House with one of the lads."

"He's on a wild goose chase," said Sergeant Campbell, hurriedly. "She's here with the girl; locked in the upstairs room. One of you get on the radio for an ambulance; I think we're going to need it, then bring all the crowbars and axes and anything else that might be useful and follow me. Fast as you can, I think she's planning to do away with the lassie."

***

Sarah's limp body landed on a large heap of smooth round stones in a sort of small rock chamber. Although she had fallen a considerable height, surprisingly, her limp unconscious state ensured that she was uninjured apart from cuts and abrasions from the rough stone. She slid down the loose heap of stones into about a foot of water. The shock of the sudden immersion roused her from unconsciousness but in her drugged state and the profound darkness, she could not grasp where she was. She lay in the water with her head resting on the bank of pebbles, drifting in and out of consciousness.

Suddenly, she came awake again as water filled her mouth and she coughed weakly. She instinctively attempted to raise herself but, almost immediately, she slipped back into unconsciousness. Several times, the same thing happened but, as the incoming tide began rapidly filling the chamber, she was gradually losing the struggle.

***

Sergeant Campbell and the two constables raced up to the tower room as fast as they could, burdened with the heavy iron levers and long axes. He examined the heavy door critically.

"We'll have to hack away the frame to give us somewhere to get the crowbars in."

Picking up an axe, he attacked the iron-hard oak. One of the constables picked up the second axe and they swung alternately at the door frame.

"I hope you're right about this, Sarge," the other constable said, watching their efforts with concern. "There's going to be all hell to pay if we've vandalised an ancient monument for nothing. Do you realise we haven't even got a warrant?"

"I know I'm right," he puffed, resting for a moment. "Anyway, don't you worry about yourself, I'll take full responsibility. It'll be my pension down the drain, not yours, if I'm wrong." Exhausted, he handed the axe to the constable. "Here, you take this and have a go, I'm worn out."

A few more blows and they had hacked two holes at the edge of the door. Dropping the axes, they inserted the crowbars and heaved. The door creaked a little and moved slightly.

"Come on, put your backs into it," the sergeant urged and threw his weight on to one of the levers. This time there was a splitting noise and the door opened about half an inch. Through the crack, they could see the metal bar of the bolt.

"Quick, put both the bars in by the bolt and let's see if we can lever it off," he gasped.

The three men heaved on the crowbars and slowly, with the creaking sound of splitting wood, the bolt was torn from the frame.

The sergeant pushed at the heavy door and it swung open. When he found that the room was in darkness he had a moment of despair. He groped for a switch. Light flooded the room and revealed the body of Mrs Grant lying in the middle of the floor.

"Oh, my God, where's the lassie?" he said. "Quick, you two start looking. I'll start here, you look in the other rooms. Go fast, she may still be alive."

He glanced over to the chest, half hoping to see it closed but the lid stood open as usual against the wall. He crossed the room to Mrs Grant's body. She was still breathing. He turned her on to her back and recoiled as her saw her face. Her skin was an awful grey, but it was her eyes. They were wide open in an unseeing fixed stare, with an expression which looked like abject terror!

He closed his mind to the sudden shock of her appearance. "It looks like she's had a stroke or a heart attack."

Stooping, he grasped her shoulder and shook her. "Mrs Grant! Can you hear me?" The woman's faint rasping breathing was the only response.

"It's no good, I'm not going to get anything out of her," he muttered. "Where on earth is the lassie?"

***

As Sarah lay in the darkness, only vaguely aware of the rising water, it seemed she could hear a voice faintly calling her name. She moved her head slightly and her lips opened as if trying to reply. The voice seemed to get louder and more insistent.

"Sarah, Sarah."

She moved her head a little more and coughed as the cold sea water flooded into her mouth. She heard the voice very loud now.

"Sarah. Wake up, Sarah, you must wake up."

She moved her head again and mumbled. The water flooded her mouth arid nostrils and she choked violently.

"Get up, Sarah. Stand up now. You must stand up, Sarah!" the voice urged her.

Weakly, the girl began to pull at the loose pebbles with her hands; she pulled her knees up and scrabbled feebly at the pile of stones. All the time, the voice in her head urged her onward.

"Stand up, Sarah. You must stand up. Don't drown like I did, stand up!"

Whimpering to herself, she made another effort and struggled to her knees on the loose stones. Now, she could feel the rough stone side of the chamber and she began to struggle upright until she was crouching against the wall.

***

Sergeant Campbell stood for a moment longer. He flung a last despairing glance around the room, then stooped and shook Mrs Grant again. She made a small moaning sound but her eyes remained fixed in their unseeing terrified stare.

"Where have you put her?" he shouted in useless anger.

He stood up and ran from the room to join the two constables in their search. He passed the garderobe and started to descend the spiral staircase.

Suddenly, he stopped as an incredible thought began to form in his brain. Turning, he ran back up the steps and in two strides reached the alcove. Sinking to his knees, he peered into the shaft but there was only darkness. He looked around him wildly but there was no separate light in the garderobe and the light from the passage did not penetrate the depths of the shaft. Leaping to his feet he ran back along the passage to the pile of abandoned equipment at the door of the tower room. Almost sobbing with relief, he picked up the powerful emergency lantern and ran back to the shaft. Kneeling again, he put his arm as far down as he could and switched on the torch.

***

Sarah, crouching half-conscious by the wall of the shaft, opened her eyes as the light flooded the chamber. The beam of the torch shone like a ghastly spotlight on the skull of Hamish Grant and she screamed with terror.

Chapter 16

Sarah was only vaguely aware of her rescue. She had confused impressions of lights and somebody crouching by her in the chamber. She could feel herself being hauled up the shaft in a sort of harness on the end of a rope and being carried carefully down the spiral stairs in the arms of a policeman, with another going ahead to prevent them falling. Then she was placed on a stretcher and taken out to the waiting ambulance. On the journey to the hospital she was still only half awake. Sergeant Campbell sat by her and held her hand and the ambulance man sat so she could not see Mrs Grant in the other bunk.

***

Sarah awoke in the unfamiliar surroundings of a hospital room. Jean was sitting by the bed smiling anxiously and an uncharacteristically subdued Alison was sitting on a metal chair at the foot of the bed, gazing at her.

She smiled wanly and reached out with both arms. "Oh, Auntie Jean!"

Jean's eyes filled with tears and she leaned across and hugged the thin body in the white hospital gown.

"Oh, Sarah. I thought I really had lost you this time. I nearly went out of my mind. Thank God we've got you back safe and sound."

"Oh, I'm so sorry. I really am so very sorry I worried you," Sarah sobbed.

Alison began crying as well and started stroking the lump in the bedclothes where Sarah's feet were; the only part that she could reach from the bottom of the bed. Suddenly, she stood up and rushed round to the opposite side from her mother and flung herself on top of them both. The three of them clung together in a sobbing pile until they were forced to part or suffocate.

The door opened and a nurse looked in. "The patient's awake I see," she smiled. "There's another visitor for you."

Sergeant Campbell came into the room and stood looking down at Sarah with a severe, very official looking expression.

"Well, young lady, this seems to be becoming a habit, doesn't it? I think I shall have to give you an official warning. I can't spend all my time rescuing you from castles. I do have other duties to attend to, you know, and besides, it's far too wearing on my nerves. I joined the Police Force for a quiet life."

Sarah smiled at him shyly and he grinned. "How are you feeling, then?"

"A bit sore but I'm all right really."

"Serves you right for frightening us all to death," he retorted with a smile.

"Too right!" Alison agreed enthusiastically. "Do you know I've been up all night and I haven't had any breakfast. I'm starving."

"Then it's a good job I brought these." The sergeant brought his hand out from behind his back; he was holding a huge box of chocolates.

Alison took them from him. "Oh, great! I'll just open them for you, shall I?" she said to Sarah, solicitously.

Just then the nurse appeared with a breakfast tray for Sarah. "Can I offer you a cup of tea?" she asked Jean.

"Yes, please," said Alison eagerly.

Alison helped herself to most of Sarah's breakfast and drank her tea.

Jean sipped hers gratefully. "I telephoned your father in New York during the night," she told Sarah. "I had a bit of trouble calming him down but I managed to convince him that you're safe. He's booked on a flight to Prestwick later today and will be here in the morning."

"Dad's coming home as well," said Alison excitedly. "Mum phoned and told him about all the trouble we've been having with you and he says he's coming to sort you out."

Sergeant Campbell made a throat clearing noise to attract attention. "If I can just change the subject a minute," he began, "I've had a word with the ward sister and she tells me you're fit to go home after the doctor's rounds. I'm afraid I'll have to take a statement from you again, so I suggest I come and see you at home this evening." He turned to Jean. "If that's convenient to you, Mrs Frazer?"

Jean nodded; suddenly everyone had stopped smiling, remembering why they were all gathered together in the hospital.

The sergeant stood up and retrieved his cap from the bed. "Well, I'd better get back to Kilmore. Heaven knows what a field day the sheep rustlers have been having while I've been otherwise engaged."

"Mr Campbell," Sarah said, shyly, "I haven't thanked you for saving me."

He stood smiling down at her. "Just to see you safe and sound is all the thanks I need, my bonny girl. If I'd been blessed with a daughter, I would have wanted her to be just like you." He turned away and left the room without another word.

***

The sergeant arrived at the house just after dinner and Alison showed him into the sitting room where Sarah was lying on the sofa in her dressing gown. After he had accepted a cup of coffee, he asked Sarah to tell him all that had happened to her.

"It was after I drank the coffee that I felt funny and couldn't stand up," she finished.

"We found a bottle of sleeping pills in the kitchen," he told her. "It's pretty certain she crushed some up and put them in your coffee."

"What I don't understand," Jean said, "is how she happened to come along just when Sarah had her burst tyre?"

"It can only have been pure coincidence," he answered. "We think that when she read the article in the Sunday paper, she panicked and made arrangements to leave the country, possibly for good, but the fact that she didn't leave for a week makes me think she was planning to get hold of Sarah and remove what she regarded as a witness, if she possibly could. The fact that you and I saw to it she wasn't left alone spoiled her plan until that very last day. In the event, Sarah just happened to be in the wrong place at the right time and she took her opportunity."

"Why did you go to the castle?" Alison asked curiously.

"Well, after you two told me what Willie Jamieson had said and then Sarah's vision of the murder, I went out to Glenmore and had a long talk with Willie. He was sure Mrs Grant had done away with Hamish but what with the family's wealth and influence, none of his superiors would entertain the idea and he was told to forget about it.

"As soon as your mother told me Sarah had gone, I knew I had to look either at Kilmore House or the castle. If I'd appreciated the workings of a deranged mind a bit better, I think I'd have tried the castle first, instead of wasting time going to the house. You see, she'd made Hamish disappear into thin air and got away with it and so she tried the same thing again with Sarah."

"Flushed her down the loo you mean," Alison shrieked with laughter.

Jean glared at her.

"Where is she now?" Sarah asked nervously.

"Mrs Grant died in hospital this morning," he answered gently. "Don't worry, she can't bother you ever again. Apparently, she'd been having treatment for high blood pressure for some years. I suppose all the stress and the fantastic effort she must have made to get you up into the tower caused her to have a stroke of some sort."

"I wonder why she did it; murder Hamish I mean," said Jean.

"Oddly enough, I can tell you," he said. "She recovered consciousness for a little while before she died and they called me in to try and get a statement from her, so obviously I asked her about that night.

"You have to remember that the fifteenth of June nineteen forty was barely a week after Dunkirk. Hamish's ship had been involved in the evacuation of the army and he'd come home on a short leave. Most people, at the time, thought it would only be a matter of weeks before Germany invaded Britain. Hamish was determined that he didn't want to see the estate taken over by some German general or Nazi politician. He had the idea of splitting up the estate and giving it away to the tenants so that they would not end up as slaves to some Nazi landlord. He had already issued instructions to the family lawyers to draw up the necessary documents.

"Mrs Grant, who'd only married him for the old family name and the estate anyway, was furious and determined to stop him. They had an almighty row about it; she killed him with the candlestick and put his body in the garderobe. Then she cleared the room up and threw his uniform and suitcase into the loch so as to make it look as though he'd gone back to his ship."

"But, what about all the blood?" asked Alison ghoulishly.

"It was mostly on the rug and the bedspread and she simply washed them in the bath. Don't you remember Annie Logan noticed that they were damp in the morning?"

Sarah shivered. "I think he was still alive when she put him down there and he drowned when the tide came in."

Sergeant Campbell nodded. "It's quite possible, although we'll never know for sure."

Sarah gazed into the distance, remembering Hamish Grant's sad voice, pleading for her help.

"Still, he's at peace now. I know I shan't hear from him again."

The End.